THE CURTAIN OF TREES

THE CURTAIN
OF TREES

S T O R I E S

Alberto Alvaro Ríos

University of New Mexico Press Albuquerque

Library of Congress Cataloging-in-Publication Data

Rios, Alberto.

The curtain of trees : stories / Alberto Rios. — 1st ed.

p.   cm.

ISBN 0-8263-2070-8

ISBN 0-8263-2071-6 (pbk.)

1. Mexican Americans—Social life and customs—Fiction.

2. Mexico—Social life and customs—Fiction.   I. Title.

IN PROCESS PS3568.I587 C

813′.54—dc21   98–58133

CIP

ACKNOWLEDGMENTS

Some stories appeared in earlier versions

in the following publications:

Clackamas Review, "The Orange Woman, the Walnut Girl"

Glimmer Train, "Nogales and the Bombs"

Hayden's Ferry Review, "The Other League of Nations"

Marlboro Review, "Salt Crosses in Doorways"

Mid-American Review, "Nine Quarter-Moons"

Ploughshares, "Outside Magdalena, Sonora"

Prairie Schooner, "Don Gustavo,

Who Had a Hand for an Ear"

I want to thank the editors of these journals,

the early readers of this manuscript,

and Arizona State University.

For Refugio Martínez Barron

AND IN MEMORY OF

Refugio, Matilde, and Consuelo Cano

"A green parrot is also a green salad and a green parrot.

He who makes it only a parrot diminishes reality.

A painter who copies a tree blinds himself to the real tree.

I see things otherwise. A palm tree can become a horse."

Pablo Picasso, from A PALM TREE BECOMES A HORSE, *1950*

CONTENTS

THESE STORIES, as I imagine and have remembered them and as they have been told to me, are about the Arizona border with Mexico at the middle of this century. They are stories from a time-between-times about people who inhabit what is a place-between-places, physically, emotionally, and historically.

The crude, ten-foot, pseudo-Berlin wall that separates the two countries now in Nogales is a good bookmark for these stories. It is a ferociously low-tech reminder that this world was, and largely still is, from a time before the great advances of science, before computers and television. These technologies exist here, of course, but they exist equally as they always have, still alive in their earlier-twentieth-century incarnations as beliefs and rituals regarding what to do in life, neighbors talking to neighbors for the real news, and the human drama of simple living—all in the face, once again, of a rapidly approaching, and rapidly passing, New World. This New World has offered so few solutions to this place that the people, as the people always have, move themselves forward—at a rate of speed and a measure of time and a definition of forward that is all their own.

I come from a family that has known this place for a long time. My favorite gauge of how this kind of life has been lived has always been my two great-aunts, Matilde and Consuelo—whom we called Connie. Two of my grandmother's sisters, they are both dead now but lived long lives dating to the last century. For all this time they lived in the region, as did their parents before them, on both sides of the border and from the time before fences. They lived judiciously and worked hard, never marrying and so making their lives together. When I was young, they were the ones who took care of their mother, my great-grandmother, but after she died, their lives, it seems, were already set. They went about thereafter taking care of each other, even if—after sixty or seventy or eighty years—they might have seemed a little edgy with each other sometimes.

Matilde was older and rounder and in her final years had a halo of white-gray-blue hair that caught the glint of Noxzema shine from her face and from her smile. As the oldest she was in charge, but Connie—who was thin and tall and angular—had her own time and her own way in conversations. For many years they lived with my great-grandmother in a house at the top of Torres Street, which was knocked down to make the freeway entry point to the border crossing. It was a house that had what seemed like a hundred back rooms, and it is in the memory of those rooms that much of this writing has been anchored. Listening to my aunts gave me the world of story, and those back rooms held its echo.

The two women later moved to another house, and they brought much of the heart of the big house with them, though at the price of sadness. It is here that I could go on too long, but I want to tell one thing, something Connie told me.

On one of our last visits before she died, Connie was in a mood I had not seen before. Matilde was talking, but Connie went to the old record player, which was disguised as a big piece of furniture. Matilde frowned and said something, but Connie continued. She wanted us to hear something, that's all, and so all right, said Matilde, though she was exasperated.

Connie put on a record and said she just wanted us to hear it because she liked it so much. The singer's name, she said, was Engelbert Humperdinck, and she pronounced it pretty well.

We listened for a while, until Matilde finally made her turn it off, but we all agreed that was a nice record. Our words made Connie smile.

And that was that. My two great-aunts, who moved from the family ranch and the hardscrabble realities of the many-sided Mexican Revolution to the songs of Engelbert Humperdinck. They showed me something about the nature of possibility. They showed me something about the real meaning and true height of the ten-foot wall.

ONE

❧ Nine Quarter-Moons ❧

The wind blew, easily enough but riling the town's bluish dust into a dry mist, which then hovered along the streets and over the gardens. The day was uncommon, and therefore unsettling. This was what people felt even though, along with the dust, the wind kept the smells of the orange blossoms and the jasmine aloft more than usual, making the blue dust smell good. Fifty-one out of fifty-two weeks a year this town was a quiet place, but for one week when the wind blew in late summer, nobody could say what would happen.

Sometimes the whole year would pass agreeably without any wind at all, and sometimes a whole decade. But this was worse, because the people in the town would start to forget. The wind, however, did not fail them over the centuries, even if they hoped otherwise. And when it did arrive for its visit of days, it came without any warning at all. Townspeople who had been through this before had to remind everyone, and had to warn the children especially, as the bully air barged into town after being away. They had so much wanted to forget that they did, in fact, forget.

The wind was not unfamiliar in its behavior, however, and behaved not unlike a person. Its coming was the kind of ordeal with which every family was familiar: everyone had experienced the unexpected appearance of a distant, barely tolerated second cousin whose uneven presence and irritating laugh through the years of occasional visits caused some tension, even if out of politeness everybody smiled.

One sat more stiffly in the living room chairs on these occasions, whether there was reason to or not. The sense of these days was, using even the simplest of gauges—the wind—that today was not like yesterday in this place and would not be like tomorrow. Today was something on its own. Sitting stiffly in a chair was a preparation. If the wind had come, who knew what else might also happen.

For some, the coming of the wind was indeed confused with the coming of a cousin, as the wind brought with it everything the cousin did: a top hat, some towels, a toothbrush, some socks. They did not come in the same order, perhaps, as the cousin might have worn them, but they were there just the same.

The wind was only a parable for what might happen in this town, but this was a town that believed in its stories. Because it came without warning, and loudly, and because of its relative scarcity, the wind was news. It was an emergency. It was a stranger. The wind might be dressed up as a cousin, but it could not give to the people on whose doors it knocked the right names of their common great-grandparents, which anybody in the family would know. That was the thing about wind, and the way to find it out. It always said Don Alfonso when the right name was Don Margarito.

The wind's arrival meant change. It was a visit where there had not been a visit yesterday. It was everything people feared, though the wind did not by itself do very much damage. Some ocotillos would fall over and some mesquites would lean, a few sheds would lose their roofs, a cat would disappear, but that was it. The wind in this town was loud but did not really itself amount to very much.

It's what was inside the wind that meant everything. It's what was inside the noise that scared everyone. It's what the wind was thinking behind the thick glasses the wind always wore that was scary. The glasses were a new trick. But why shouldn't the wind, after all, wear glasses? It had seen everyone else do so, and they were easily enough taken off a careless face.

The glasses by design let the wind see everything more closely. But as the people looked through the glasses in reverse, the optical effect made the wind seem farther away. So when they turned to go, the wind was suddenly upon them, just like that. It was an accidental deception, a by-product of science. This, of course, was just one more thing that made science suspect in this town.

But though the wind was news, it also brought news. Inside itself the wind was full of newspapers and book leaves. People here enjoyed learning about family in distant towns and about what the government was up to—up to yet again. But what the wind carried was not that kind of news, though at first it might have seemed to be, as the wind sometimes pushed a few pages along the street, inviting enough to the casual reader.

Much more than that, the wind in its suddenness and largeness had inside itself old radios, and the fizzing tubes that went into them, which were suddenly alive and electrical in the whirling, friction energy of the wind's sometimes circular, sometimes rowing motions, so that voices would come out of the air when the wind was strongest. The echoes of conversation from other towns also came out of it, and the occasional cat and mesquite branch and swirling parrot, which, angry at the spinning but even more angry to have gone so long without dinner, repeated such vocabularies as were known to it and some that were not. These parrots in their squawking anger simply started to make up words and string them into sentences.

All of this was unnerving to the town, which was otherwise a nice town, and quiet. At first, some of the townspeople would let this pretend cousin in. It was a good disguise, people said later, but too late. Opening up the front door to this impostor was a mistake, and the wind would enter, but like a thief, taking everything there was to take into its hundred arms and running out the back door before the owners of the house could even finish closing the front door.

The townspeople would go chasing this outlaw, which ran bold as anything through the back alleys with its treasure of toasters and wooden frames and feather pillows. Before long, the wind was a circus wind, holding so many high-wire acts, cannon smoke, screams, and elephants. The elephants were really just large cardboard boxes but, when viewed through squinted eyes and through the dust, they were dark and lumbering, with their various flaps taking on the aspects of a trunk or some tusks, and sometimes a curling tongue.

It was a circus, but the ticket was expensive. Still, who did not go? The wind gathered the townspeople and dazzled them. By now it had assembled them all under its tent and made them into an audience. It made them gasp and spat at them with confetti. It roared, but that was the easiest trick of all. Even a third-rate wind can roar.

What this wind did, however, was to save the best for last. In the confusion of townspeople, who themselves were the best of clowns, running this way and that, up and down stairs, tripping and bumping into one another, and with hats turned around and clothes filled with air so as to make them look fat—in this confusion the wind would do its greatest trick.

In a smell of cotton candy, which was really orange blossoms and jasmine, with perhaps some honeysuckle and chicken with rosemary that had been cooking; in a dappled light, which had to filter through all the things swirling in the air, and which got turned left and right, and which sometimes filtered through colored glass or cellophane, turning blue and red and violet; in a taste of rain, not so much because rain was imminent but because so many bottles of water and apple soda had been opened by the wind, along with so many cartons of milk and tins of gasoline and barrels of beer, which became a wet gold in the air; in an aura of Neapolitan ice cream strategies, a taste of watermelon welded to a taste of butter and wedded as well to a taste of rabbit stew; and in a roar, but a roar at once taken back as too amateurish and easy, so that all that was left was quiet: in this quiet, the wind found its moment and disappeared.

Whole reckless menageries came crashing down, bags of groceries and the bicycles that had been delivering them, errant shoes and lost earrings, a barber pole, all manner of worldly life.

But no one paid attention. They were not prepared. The towns-people in that moment should have known what would happen next and been ready, some of them having been through this, after all, for a half century. But they were not.

The wind just went, and left them with no more of a thank-you card than a phone call announcing its arrival.

The moment was so sudden that the wind, in the style of the circus it brought, could have vanished in a cloud of smoke. But it was itself the smoke, and the dust that had helped make the wind began to fall gently onto the ground.

The falling particles covered the townspeople in a clean, dry snow, a flour comprised of everything around them that had been ground by the wind into dust and lifted up. It was a flour of their lives, tinged a little with blue, and it made them all look like they had gray hair and old milk on their upper lips.

Their aspect reminded them all of the baker, who often looked like a ghost after working with flour all day, and whose sign of hard work was not dirt under his fingernails like everybody else but a whiteness, nine quarter-moons. He had lost one finger when he was the butcher, but this only made him a more careful baker, and the people trusted him. To give up a finger for this town counted for something.

Everybody agreed he was a better baker than a butcher, any-way. The thing was, his finger was never found. In a cookie or a pastry, it would have been obvious, but in a white packet of meat, with a little bit of blood on it—his decision to become a baker had been a good decision all around.

But a dust particle or a chair, it didn't matter what fell around them now. They were numb and without feelings, without fear. As the wind's sound left, they began to make their own. Their movements around town combined into a quiet, if harsh, sym-phony, a dull music. As they started to pick things up, to regather the chickens and all the rest, the strains of the song of hand and muscle were familiar, an old music of syncopated sighs as much as things. It was the sound of ancient work. Fix the fence, sweep the floors, paint the door blue again.

The wind was gone and the gathering and cleaning up began right away, and the town became the town once more. The wind's visit all happened so fast, it seemed not to have happened, and cleaning up quickly seemed the only right thing to do. A visitor passing through after these days would not have believed this story of the wind and its spectacle, and cleaning up quickly was a way not to have to explain.

All this is true, and explains something about what happened next.

Two days after the wind departed, Mr. Calderón's second cousin from Hermosillo showed up for a visit, unannounced. Hat and suitcase in one hand, while the other hand adjusted his thick spectacles, this cousin knocked, thinking it odd all the while that the town was so quiet. He had walked from the bus stop and not passed a soul.

But people saw him. Inside their houses, as they cleaned and happened to be near windows and breezeways, various townspeople saw the man walking in the street and sent their husbands or their oldest daughters next door to pass the word, this passing of the word walking—as it invariably does—at a pace faster than the man's.

The door bolt moved right away at the sound of the knock, and almost before.

"We've been expecting you," said Mr. Calderón. He opened the door and let the man in, but set his jaw in a frown as the visitor passed.

The man entered, smiling despite his cousin's demeanor and trying to put a shine on his arrival. As he entered the front room, the crowd of twenty or thirty people he encountered was absolutely quiet, though he was startled and immediately made the sign of the cross.

"Dios mío," he said, and waited for something to happen, for someone to say something or give him some explanation.

They said nothing and just looked at him, hard. If there were thirty townspeople in that room, then sixty eyes focused themselves in this moment on this man.

The sign of the cross, it was a good show, a reassuring reflex and a comforting demonstration, but they would not be fooled. This was not nearly enough.

Mr. Calderón, his jaw still set in its frown, approached this man and asked him the question they had all come to ask.

On the visitor's answer the fate of this day depended, and they made him speak it slowly into the microphone, which is how they held the town's biggest broom menacingly up to his face.

"So," said Mr. Calderón, taking a deep breath, "if it is you, what is the name of our grandfather?"

Two

Outside Magdalena, Sonora

The waiter called me over from my table with a wave. It was a wave first with his hand, but then with his eyebrow and his smile, and with a nod of his head to be sure. He called me over more with these than with his hand, and so I got up. In an unfamiliar place, one pays attention. One uses for ears the eyes as well.

But this attentiveness was not for much. The waiter, who turned out to be the owner, was simply occupied with washing glasses and didn't want to be bothered with coming over to my table. He thought I was the good sort and that I wouldn't mind, he said. So he had taken the chance that I would not be offended. And anyway, a person always took a chance one way or another with strangers, didn't I think so?

He looked at me up and down with his bigger eye. He did it in such a manner that I knew I need not answer his question. That eye also said it had not seen me around here before. But if he indeed said anything aloud, his words were muffled behind the plate he was drying by blowing on it. He had done the same with each of the glasses, a shake, a little drying, and then blowing.

The rhythm of it all should have been comforting, but it was not. It said instead that the waiter, the owner, knew what to do, and I did not. I had the menu, but he knew what to do with the glasses.

The place was open-air after entering, a restaurant and a bar and a coffeehouse all in one. Just behind and to the side of him was an opening to a garden, a whole wall missing, but leading to tables surrounded by bougainvillea and ivy.

Without turning to see where I was glancing, he said to me,

"It's very beautiful, don't you think? Everyone goes to sit out there. And why not? Except for the bees, and sometimes the wasps, it's perfect. I put up some nets for shade. Do you like them?"

I nodded my head even though I couldn't see them. I could only see the shade. "It looks very nice," I said. I was a little embarrassed as the words stayed a little too long in my mouth.

I had come here to this town in Sonora from Arizona, and my Spanish was good but certainly not perfect. It's just what had happened through the years and between generations. But we came from the small towns here, in the middle and in the north of Sonora, Rayón and Cucurpe, San Ignacio, towns like this one. I was in the right place.

"Then that is where you should sit. Come on." He wiped his hands on his apron, got what seemed to be a menu different from what I was holding, and began to lead me out to the garden. Maybe it was in English, but I hoped not.

I had not seen the garden area on first entering, and yet now it seemed to hold the entire place. I had looked only straight ahead in this place, and not to the right or to the left.

He stopped when I didn't quite follow, looking at my first table and the notebook I had left lying there.

"Oh, don't worry, I'll bring it," he said, but it wasn't enough. He could tell. "Oh, and don't worry, there are no bees right now. No bees and no wasps. It's not the season."

I started to follow him. I hadn't meant to be stubborn, and my standing motionless had been only a small moment, but it's true that I had just stood there.

"You'd know that if you were from here," he said, "no bees right now," and he walked to the garden without looking back.

I retrieved the notebook myself and followed him to the garden tables, which were quiet and cool in the netted midmorning light. The sun was on the other side of the building's roof, and the birds were happy. He stood by a table and nodded to it.

I sat, but in pulling out my chair made the noise of a chair being pulled out. It's not much, but unmistakable as a noise. Some birds flew, and the nets moved a little. He had gotten the netting strung up high, over the tops of the umbrella trees, but with some netting under them as well to catch the yellow seed balls. One fell through and bounced simply off the brick floor into the garden.

"It's too early for lunch," he said to me. "Maybe you want some coffee? Some *pan dulce?* It's fresh?"

Everything he said had a question mark, but nothing was a question. He was already starting to walk back inside. I would have stopped him, but he was right.

STRANGERS had passed through town before, of course, he said. Most were confused or nervous, but some took control. Some strangers were stronger than others.

"They're the ones." He looked at me again, with that up-and-down glance, and again with his larger eye. But this time his look was a joke, and we laughed.

"I understand," I said, and I meant it. They're the ones to look out for, I supposed he was saying. I was a stranger here, after all, but I hadn't thought much of it, not in those terms. I was a stranger to this town, it was true, but I understood what he said. Be careful.

That connected us a little in the moment, enough so that when he came back with the coffee and sweet bread he sat down and joined me.

He didn't ask if I minded, and I didn't mind, but it surprised me anyway.

"You can recognize a stranger in this town, and not because he is a stranger," said the man, and took a drink of his coffee even though it looked very hot, with enough steam to look like the hands of a ghost reaching up for him. "It won't be the person at all. Not at all. It will be how others in town treat him." With that he nodded his head, and it seemed to be him, though it might as easily have been the hands of the ghost making him nod like a puppet.

I thought about him sitting down with me so readily. It was, after all, friendly, but a little odd too. This didn't seem to be what one would do with a stranger, here or anywhere else. He was acting like a friend, and I didn't know why.

Though why should there be a why? I thought. I should feel good. Still, I wasn't so sure. The whole thing was confusing.

"A stranger here, well, this is someone accorded the utmost in civility. Civility and suspicion, with nothing in between," he said with a laugh. "I think we treat our strangers better than ourselves."

I supposed it was funny too, and I smiled a little with him. But I was sitting in an awkward chair and could not decide what to make of him or of myself. Was I the stranger or not? He gave me no time to think. This was perhaps a friendly act, not allowing me the moment it takes for cynicism to build a crust around a conversation and then between two people.

Either he was indeed being friendly or else in fact I was the stranger, and he was keeping me off balance. I shrugged my shoulders, finally, to which he nodded his head. It was as if our bodies were themselves talking.

"Well, you know," he said to me, "a stranger in this town cannot simply order a meal, eat it, and be gone. The owner, well— you know, the other owners in the other places—they instead will offer this person, this stranger, the entire menu, no charge today, and a free tequila to boot. Just like that, no joke."

I looked at him. "A free choice? On the house?" Mine were real question marks.

"Not just a free choice, my friend. The whole meal. Anything on the menu." He nodded his head *yes*.

"I don't understand." Perhaps, I thought, it was the ghost talking, the ghost of the coffee, all steam. Maybe more than hands had entered and moved him.

"The whole menu. How will the owner know what the stranger wants if he doesn't offer him everything?" He looked at me for some sign of common sense but threw up his hands. Just a little. It was not a rude gesture, but this small throwing up of his hands said what he felt.

"Listen," he continued. "I might offer the stranger simply a pork chop and offer to cook it any way he pleased, and he would say thank you and eat it with a smile. But in his heart he would still be thinking about the tacos, and he would leave unhappy, even though he is made to smile, because what he really wanted was the tacos.

"But a free pork chop, how could he pass it up? And then what will he say to others?" With that he threw up his hands again, but not in frustration. It was more of a *ta da*, there you are, it's as plain as the nose on your face.

I lifted my own eyebrows.

"No, my friend," he said, clearly understanding this conversation enough for the both of us. "No. Strangers cannot be trusted. That is why I offer them anything they want. For free. Absolutely. I don't want them to say bad things about me. Who knows what that would mean?" He nodded his head, not one way or the other, but it moved.

"I see," I said, but I was just being polite. I didn't really see at all.

"Well, it is a good thing, then. Take us, for instance. I haven't seen you around here before, but since you understand, now I know I can trust you.

"So then, will you want some lunch? It's not too expensive. I'll make some tacos. After the sweet breads you don't want anything too heavy. I'll go make some?"

With that he was gone, and I was left with my cooler coffee. I hadn't planned to stay for lunch, but now I was obligated. I wasn't sure how I was obligated, exactly, but I was sure that I was.

WHEN THE owner brought the tacos out, I asked him how he knew I would like them.

"But who doesn't?" he said, and went off to serve the others who were now gathering in the restaurant.

That seemed to be that.

I had come to town to look for family, for ancestors, really, and this man, Don Francisco as it turns out, would have been a perfect starting point. But what I was doing here never came up. He never quite asked me, and I never quite said.

I had thought to tell him in the beginning, when he gave me a chance in the conversation, but then I thought the better of it. He was too good a starting point. I knew he would know.

That was the problem. He seemed to know everything, and I wasn't sure I liked that. He made it all easy, and it was easy, and should have been easy, but still, when something actually works that way, you get suspicious.

I don't know how to explain myself in that moment, but that other language was at work between us. It was my body talking. And it never asked Don Francisco about my family. It would ask somebody else. That's all there was to it, whether I agreed with my body or not. The words just never came out.

I should stop for a moment and say that I liked the man a great deal, and I liked this place. It was all, in its way, perfect. And what went into my mouth in this late morning was more arresting than anything I could bring out.

The tacos were fine, crisp with good meat. The salsa, I could taste, was something made today, and fit the taste of the tacos like a meeting of primary colors, a perfect blue and a perfect yellow making a fine green. It was elemental and sure, this taste and this meal, a small alchemy with each bite.

Maybe I was just hungry, or maybe the embrace of the trees and the treble notes of the birds affected me more than I could know, but this food simply tasted sound. Complete. There was nothing else to say. This couch needed no doily. I was tired and I sat down and I felt good. That's the kind of tacos they were.

I HAD WORK to do, however, and could not stay here all day. Nothing was making me leave, and I had no real desire to leave, and I suspected I would just be coming back, but *I have work to do* is just the kind of thing one says anyway. Who knows why? It was just time to go.

Don Francisco had by this time already brought me two Tecates with lime and another coffee. I was enjoying myself too much. That was the thing.

"How much do I owe you?" I asked him as he passed by. He stopped and added something on his fingers.

"Eleven dollars, American."

"Eleven," I repeated, and started to move my hand to my wallet. *Eleven*, said my brain, was not too cheap, but neither was it the most I had ever paid.

My body echoed, *Eleven*, but didn't understand one way or the other. It would have paid any amount of money for those two hours of life. But it was my body as well telling me to leave.

I pushed my chair out, making that sound of chairs again, but this time it felt right. It was a rhyme sound, so that if the first moment had begun my visit here, then this sound ended it. I paid Don Francisco the eleven dollars and left another dollar and a half on the table.

He said thank you with a nod and I walked out of the restaurant. I thought I was a stranger walking into the place, but it looked like I had to pay for my meal anyway. On the one hand, that should have made me feel good. That I was a friend.

On the other hand, there was no other hand. Don Francisco was sitting on it.

Still, the time had come for doing what I had come to do. I walked into the street to cross it, but I turned and looked back at the restaurant. It was called *El Primo*. I stood there looking at the sign until a car honked at me and made me jump back onto the sidewalk in front of the restaurant.

El Primo. It can mean "the first," or "the foremost," or anything like that. But it also means "the cousin." And in that moment my whole lunch shouted up to me from my stomach. It was not a bad shout, but it was a noise.

It was some chemistry, some magnetism. My body knew. If

opposites attract, similars repel. This is what my body felt, even if my brain thought otherwise. This is why I felt I had to leave. My body felt the greater thing. It knew pure and simple this man was my family.

Oh no, I thought before anything else, but I didn't know why I thought that. I just knew it was the right thing to think. The two words rhymed like the pulling out and pushing in of the chair. *Oh no* and *Don Francisco.* They were the fitting words, all right. Not reasonable, but absolute. Something indeed from magnetism.

I should have been happy, of course. Everything in the bar had been wonderful. Don Francisco was a charming host, and, perhaps, along his lines of reasoning, a friend of sorts already. This was a good day. A good morning turning into a good day. I pulled myself up, took a breath to quiet my lunch, and walked straight back into the place.

But my body said, *Oh no,* louder. It said the words, and somehow they got stuck in its mouth, like a strand of food in the teeth. There was no reason for the words. But so what?

"DON FRANCISCO," I said as I entered, just as easy and as straight as words can be. "Don Francisco."

"My friend," he said, in just the same manner. We both meant them, but our bodies were shaking their heads. It wasn't a shaking side to side in a *no,* not exactly, but neither was it precisely a *yes.* It was just a shaking. Maybe it was the ghosts. Our ghosts.

"I hope I can indeed count you as my friend, Don Francisco." I cleared my throat. "I need your help."

"Whatever I can do, of course," he said, very quickly.

It was hard for me to believe his answer. It seemed as if he had not had time to digest what he had heard. That he had given his answer just as a reflex, *a sus órdenes.* At your service. Just like that. The way he would say to anybody.

"Don Francisco, am I a stranger to you?" I asked him just in this way because I didn't know how else to begin.

"Well, no, we're old friends now, aren't we? And you did pay your bill, after all. We don't let strangers do that, do we?"

"Don Francisco, please listen. I have something serious to ask."

"Of course you might be that kind of stranger who pays his bill just to throw me off the track. That might be." He cocked his head.

"Don Francisco, I'm looking for my family."

He raised his arms as if to hug me. "Son!"

He said this and then started laughing. It made me take a small step backward.

But he waved me back toward him. "It's just that you look so serious," he said, and stopped the joke. "All right, tell me, then, your family—when did you lose them?"

With this I let out my breath, not able to get him to understand because I wanted to say everything at once, but all the words together did not fit through the mouth. I made a small sound instead. But he understood, and he walked me to a near table, pulling out a chair. There was the sound again, but this time almost clean, almost exactly what had come out of me.

"I've come to look for family. Ancestors. Cousins. Anybody. Like that. Do you know what I mean?" The real words in order sounded anticlimactic. Why was that so difficult to say? I wondered. And to a stranger, after all. That was the truth of it.

"Oh, sure, I understand perfectly," said Don Francisco. "Ancestors." He pointed to some pictures hung in a corner of the room, toward the end of the counter, along with a picture of the Virgin and John Kennedy and the old pope, John.

"Like those," he said. "I have plenty. Do you want some?"

"Don Francisco, listen. I do want some. It's not a joke. I've come all the way to find out. My Spanish is maybe not so good, I know, but I come from the Calderón family—do you know them?" I looked at him with my eyes, but I could tell that my eyes were already doing their own work. They told him I was serious. Eyes can be used, but they have a mind of their own.

"Okay. I understand. I myself am Francisco Ríos de Calderón. I know the family as well as I know my mother, God bless her."

"Stop it, Don Francisco, please." I didn't want him to tease me, not anymore.

"It's true, though. That's who I am."

"Well," I said, looking at him a little harder, "I know the family has a Francisco."

"Doesn't every family?" He laughed again in spite of everything. Don Francisco had a helper who must have come to work just in the few minutes I had gone out of the restaurant, and Don Francisco signaled him to bring us some beers.

"But I don't think it's me you're looking for. I'm Ríos de Calderón. You're talking about Francisco Calderón, just like that, on his father's side, not his mother's side like me."

"Oh," I said. It was all I could think of. When the beer came, I took a good drink. I noticed when the helper opened them, a kind of steam came out of the beer too, as with the coffee. A spray, and then a steam, something out of the cold. What is with this place? I thought.

"I was named after him, though. Don Pancho was my uncle, I think. You know, it was so long ago, uncle or cousin, it was something like that. Do you know what I mean?" Don Francisco took a drink of his own beer.

"Would that make us cousins, then? Or something?" I had come to the right place after all.

"Well, I count as cousins those who aren't about to ask me for something."

"I just want to know more. That's all."

"They all say that, my friend. I would have thought the less of you if you did not lie to me a little like that. I think you have just been promoted. But all right. I'll tell you something.

"The chairs and tables outside. They're from my house when I was growing up. Your grandmother and grandfather sat in them. Your *nana* and *tata*. In fact, it was your *nana's* hairnet, the one she always wore after your *tata* died, that gave me the idea for what to do in the garden outside."

With that he began to talk a little faster. It was the beer, the good coldness of the beer, or me, or the remembering of the detail—whatever it was, it made him talk faster. I couldn't follow everything, but when I was stuck, he put his hand on my arm and got a big smile on his face. It was okay.

"And the salsa, did you like it? That was hers. I learned it from her. She used to make it many years ago when I first opened this place."

"Yes, wonderful, Don Francisco, it's wonderful. What else can you tell me?" I really was smiling. Something was letting go, something I could feel.

Don Francisco said a few more things, pointing to an old hat rack and some curtains. Then we got up to look at the pictures.

"She was beautiful," he said, and pointed at my grandmother. "I don't have any pictures of the *señor* here. Maybe tonight we'll find one."

I looked at the picture. She was beautiful, despite the wan curtain used as background. I had seen enough of these pictures by now to recognize how the photographers would use anything as backdrop regardless of its condition. What mattered was the subject, of course. And there she was, in a jet satin hat and some lipstick, which had been colored in.

"That's not her," I said.

Don Francisco looked at me. "What do you mean? Look again. Maybe you've seen some other pictures of her and she just looks different here. That's it. Look in this light over here," he said, and took the picture off its hanger to hold it up to the window.

"No, it's not." I looked at it for a long time. There was no question.

"But you've tricked me," said Don Francisco. He looked at me hard, with edges. He didn't want to look at me that way, I could tell, but his eyes were doing what they wanted and his bones at the joints of his elbows flexed to a point.

"No, no, Don Francisco. I didn't trick you. This just isn't her."
And it wasn't. Maybe I had explained myself badly, awkwardly,
with the wrong words. But it wasn't her. We both could see that
now.

"BUT YOU MADE me remember her. You made me tell you.
What is this all about? Who are you?" He sat back in his chair and
tried to fold his arms, but they fell out of their own knot and fell a
little into his lap. They too were doing their own work. They were
telling the truth.

As was Don Francisco. But so was I. I told him everything I
knew. And he told me everything he knew. But it wasn't right. It
was close for a long time, but it wasn't right.

We talked a little more, and I shrugged my shoulders. I hadn't
meant to upset this man who had been only kind to me. Who
could have suspected he would feel this way? Don Francisco kept
shaking his head a little in a *no*. He didn't say the word, but it's
what he meant. He had given something away, or had let me see,
something that was not mine.

He pointed me to the church. "That's where the records are,"
he said. "And over there is the cemetery. Good luck." He wished
me good luck, and he meant the words, but it was with a tem-
pered spirit.

I should have been the one to feel that way, and I did. But he
felt it so much that it crowded into me until I was feeling him
feeling this disillusionment. Disillusionment is not the right
word. It was something much bigger and spelled much smaller. It
was a real feeling more than a word.

We parted at the door to the restaurant. Afternoon had come
and was honking to take me away like a taxi. The bright afternoon light is sometimes like that, especially when you want to be
back inside taking a nap in the home of a friend. In the home of a
cousin, just for the afternoon.

"Strangers," said Don Francisco as one of his last words, but he
said the word more with his larger eye, which sometimes not only

has a mind but a voice. He said it, and then he gave a laugh. But it was only half a laugh. I wanted to make up the difference, but I couldn't.

"Well, you've been the best stranger, anyway," he said. "I played a joke on you, and you played a joke on me. Even?" It was not a real question, the same way he had done at the beginning of the day. With that he shook my hand.

"I'll see you," I said, but realized that these words might not be true. Maybe he was right, I thought, about believing strangers. He was right about everything else. What had I done to him?

I didn't know why he got so upset. I thought it was a small thing, the asking of a question and the giving of an answer, but I was wrong. I was wrong this time.

Maybe it was something in my Spanish, in the way I said or understood words. Some things don't travel well between languages. But perhaps it was simpler. Maybe it was just a gauge of meaning, so much about how he had loved this woman, and how he missed her, and tried to keep her in all of her ways.

Maybe it was as simple as that. The feeling belonged to him. And for a moment, maybe there was someone else. It happens with a lot of things.

I didn't know if I was a stranger or a friend, finally. Or what he was to me. Even though all the names were true for both of us, he wasn't finally my cousin, if you believed the church.

I didn't say anything else as we parted, of course. Just a small wave good-bye. I don't know if it was enough.

🌿 Salt Crosses in Doorways 🌿

The change was gradual, but there were signs enough. They were small, to be sure, but even a small hiccup is something of its own, and with a name for itself large enough to be ominous by any measure. I was with her from fall until spring, until she left us all as you've heard. But that's why you're here. You want to know, as they say, the real story.

There is no real story, of course. There never is. Everybody has a different story, so instead of a rose it's always a bouquet. This doesn't seem so bad unless you're a reporter or something and need to write the real story. You're in trouble then. You're not a reporter, are you?

Well, what she did, really, what her job was in her later years, was to talk. My grandmother—well, she was your grandmother too, wasn't she, as you say—she did it all the time, whether or not anybody was there to listen. That might seem strange, but sometimes an echo can seem like an answer. And since it's what a person has said, it's probably more agreeable than someone else arguing. So her talking to herself, it wasn't such a bad thing.

It's true, though, that she began to get louder and louder about everything, about bombs and coffee and the old days, but I would not be troubled. I think she was simply speaking loud enough to insert some words into the walls and ceiling, the way a squirrel puts extra food in its mouth for the winter. You know, so that when she was lonely, she could just sit sometimes and listen. It was like her own record player, this house, which was full of the loudness of her opera.

She used to talk about everything toward the end, as if she

were an accountant balancing sums. She said everything two and three times just to be sure. When she was like that, she was very good, very concentrated, so no one dared to disturb her. She had a strong face again, in those moments, a face like she used to have.

If you needed her, you could put your hand on her shoulder, and she would stir out of her state. But she wouldn't stop talking. She would say something about wherever she was in her story, whether or not you had been a party to its beginning and whether or not you would be staying for its conclusion. It took a while, sometimes, to tell her that dinner was ready.

We had all kinds of citrus, I remember her saying once when I had brought her back from where she was. But apples and pears were a luxury. Bananas weren't being brought up from the south yet, except maybe a few of the little kind, which are so sweet. There were dates. They were yellow on the trees, though, and had to be tied up with jute sacks so that they'd ripen. Otherwise they would just stay yellow. And some nuts. There were some nuts.

We ate rabbit, rabbits and hares, and chicken on Sundays. We ate some lamb, too. It was cheaper than beef then. Nobody can imagine that now, but it's true.

That's how she would talk, and her head would shake a little as she did. It was a shake out of sadness, not sickness, and I tried not to notice. She would talk about everybody she grew up with, all her cousins, and then she would wonder what happened to them all. There was always one answer: *fueron al norte*. They went to the United States. All of them, she would say, but she didn't understand the attraction.

Everybody who had gone to cross over, she knew what happened to them, she would say. Crossing over to that country was more than just being here and then being there. To begin with, over there you have to start to walk differently. It only makes sense.

Over there the ground moves one way, with its own shapes and trails and streets. It's different from here. So, however you learned to walk here would have to be different over there, or else you would fall over things. It only makes sense. And if you walk differently, then your legs and your body have to adjust, and so you begin to look different. It's simple.

And a person's eyes see different things over there, which make your eyes have to do something different as well, and so they begin to look different too.

All this is no mystery, she would say. It's easy enough to see that nobody who goes away comes back the same. And so she was never surprised at how different and how much older relatives looked when they came to visit her after a long time, and how they could not speak Spanish very well.

The eyes, the legs, the mouth, the nose: they all have to learn over, and this is what happens, she would say to me when one cousin or another left after a visit. That place makes them change into something else. That's the only way to live there.

When she tired of this, she talked about the *señorita guardada* down the road; do you know that phrase? It means a lady who has saved herself for marriage but who has perhaps waited a little too long and now finds herself in her fifties. It is a kind term for all the things that can do that to a life.

Well, this lady, Señorita Cano, who turns out to be a cousin herself, but which neither of them realized for many years, this lady, well, was always putting salt in her doorways in the shape of crosses. Who did not know that this was a good thing, of course, to ward off the devil, like painting the door of a house blue? But when a person slips to the ground on the grains of salt, at that moment it doesn't seem as smart as it did at the kitchen table when they had just talked about doing it.

That's what did it, I think. The salt cross she slipped on when she last went to visit. If you hadn't heard that she had fallen, well, I'm not surprised. She would never tell anyone because then they would think she was the devil, that the salt had caught her, and so she denied it to the end. She never fell, she would say, although it broke something in her, no matter what the doctor said. She could always fool a doctor.

Besides, she had fallen before and survived well enough. She told me a story once, about her uncle Carlos, who was a stern man, perhaps even cruel. Of course, since he was a member of the family, nobody could say as much. She said that he taught her and her sisters to swim. He tricked them this way and that until he got them to a small stream, where he made them all get in the water and start to move their arms and legs.

He hit them with a small branch from a mulberry tree over and over until they swam, even though they would come home with bruises and welts. They became good swimmers, she said, but she would set her jaw when she said it.

Then one day her uncle Carlos decided that my grandmother should not only ride a horse, but ride one very well. He enticed my grandmother, who in those days as a teenager had long hair and thick, all the way down her back, onto a large horse, and then he handed the baby Pirrín, my uncle, up into her arms. Everyone agreed, on that day and all the way to now, that Pirrín was a beautiful baby. My grandmother held him with attention and so could not hold the reins of the horse.

Uncle Carlos, with the same switch he had used to teach my grandmother and her sisters to swim, hit the haunches of the horse, and it went off at a gallop. My grandmother kept herself and the baby upright and could not have done otherwise, so much was her upbringing. Uncle Carlos laughed at first, but the others watching screamed. My grandmother made no sound, save perhaps for a low purr exchanged with the boy charged to her arms, which she kept close around him.

At a distance still within view on this ranch, which was called *la Calera*, the horse, whose own name is lost to the years, because it was unguided ran underneath a tree with low branches as some horses will to get the flies and beetles off their backs. The tree swept up my grandmother by her hair into its own arms.

The horse kept running and went on to stumble and kill itself, but my grandmother stayed hanging there, with the baby folded to her. She hung by her long, thick hair, which had tangled and wisped into the tree. She hung there and did not move, and the baby did not cry. She purred to him, she said. She purred to him with small and quiet words.

When the others came to her rescue, they had to cut her hair to get her out of the tree. She never grew it long again, and Uncle Carlos, who kept his hair very short, went on to live by himself in an orchard, which I visited once as a child. When I visited it was spring, and all the fruit in all the trees hung there spectacularly. But I also remember there was a sadness in Uncle Carlos's eyes, something, even though the taste of the peaches and apricots, of the nectarines and the lemons, the taste was everything good.

I have one picture of him, black and white, the top button buttoned on his old white shirt and his head cocked a little to the side. You know, that's who she always thought was the devil. She never said it, but it was clear. When she slipped in the doorway and it turned out that maybe she was the devil, I think this scared her. It scared her more than the fall.

A few days after this she started to say some things to me that didn't make sense then, though they do now. At the time I just thought she was rattling on the way she did sometimes, that I had caught her in the middle of something.

"Well, they say," she started to tell me, "that when you look in a mirror, you see the opposite of yourself." To think, she said, that she had liked what she had seen there in the mirror all these years. And it wasn't just how she looked. She said to me, but in a whisper now, that she also used to think that she could see goodness inside herself if she looked long enough through the little black parts in her eyes.

"But could the mirror have been showing me just the opposite of what I am? Isn't this how they say mirrors work?"

I wanted to laugh, but of course I didn't. I held her hand and told her she was getting herself all bothered for nothing. What a thing to think.

But I think that's what was inside her. I think it's what she thought—that instead of being a good person, she was in some way the devil.

She said that the way she always thought the United States changed everybody, maybe it wasn't true. Maybe she was the one who changed. Maybe it was her. After all, to tell the truth, she would say in a whisper, everybody else just seemed so happy. Oh, well, they complained, all right, but they complained about all sorts of things she had never even heard of—new kinds of ovens, computer machines, machines that make your coffee in the morning. Maybe it wasn't them at all. Maybe it was something wrong with her.

She tried to tell me more, but I started to laugh even if I didn't want to. She just came from another time, and I didn't understand. She was trying to tell me something, but she stopped herself. I didn't know how she could believe all this, but I think she did.

I had even begun to laugh about the salt crosses earlier but thought the better of it. It was all from another century. Everything was a sign to her. She learned this from her mother. And though she had once been adept at reading the long hiss of the cicadas and the rain such a sound meant, her eyes now failed her.

She might have tried to tell me how scared she was by all this again last Sunday, but I was there with my wife, so she was quiet. For her not to talk, as I've said, was unusual of course, but that day, forgive me, I enjoyed the difference.

As we sat, the whole afternoon seemed to slow down. She put out some things to eat, a couple of white wedding cookies, some dried fruit, two chocolates—little bits of this and that, as if we were children playing house. That's what I thought at the time. It was afternoon tea, with tea foods like in the books, except that it was coffee. We were adults and children at the same time.

She made a tin pot of cowboy coffee, like on the *rancho*, she said, from memory. From childhood. We all laughed a little. In the old way, she pinched the coffee up in her hands and not in a spoon and made the fire on the stove from a match. We sat with her and talked, but the talk was like the bits of food, a little of this and something from that other plate, always with a napkin and a thank-you.

We sat and visited and watched her take small drinks from her cup until the afternoon light was funny in the room, and then we said our good-byes. The visit was a liniment applied to the hard day, in the quiet of its language and the lifting of her small, china cups to our lips. It was simplicity, and held only what it needed. It was a gentle visit, and we did not see her again.

❧ Nogales and the Bombs ☙

I was five years old, which isn't so important all by itself, but it was 1929, or maybe 1930. This was a big time in the world. I was living in Nogales, Sonora, with my parents. I don't remember if it was a weekday or a weekend, or even if it was winter or summer, but I do remember the hour when everything happened.

In those days my mother would get us all up at 7:00, and we would eat cereal, eggs, or sweet bread and invariably milk. It wasn't so different from now. We always wanted coffee, but coffee, my mother said, would make us sick. Our drink was milk. Or something like milk, anyway. Sometimes to make milk my mother would put Eagle condensed milk in water. It might not have been Eagle brand, but it had an eagle on it. This had vitamins, she said. But the truth is, it was cheaper than milk, and some days this made a difference.

But it was the coffee we wanted. My mother used to make the coffee herself. It was called *caracolillo,* and she learned how to make it on the *rancho* she grew up on. *Caracolillo* was made of pea beans, not coffee beans, but it still had a good taste, and it was still called coffee. A lot of people drank the already made Café Combate, but not us. My mother would roast the beans, which were small, and then she would grind them.

First she would light a match and turn on the stove. Then she would put a big pan on the stove. She would put the *caracolillo* beans in dry and then stir them around so that they wouldn't burn. As she was stirring she would put sugar on the beans, and it would stick to them, making a kind of skin. When the heat changed them from green to black, my mother would pick up a bean with her fingers and snap it in half. That's how she would know if it was done, although I couldn't tell one way or the other. I was still too young.

Then quickly she would pick up the pan and dump out all the beans onto a clean tablecloth. She'd leave the beans there to cool and to dry. When they were ready, she would put them in a large jam jar and seal them tight. Whenever she wanted to make coffee, she had a small grinder, which you had to hold between your knees. I had to do it, and I hated it because it was real work and it hurt my legs. But I would grind the beans, and the powder would fall into a small box at its base.

The fire and the beans and the sugar and the grinding—it all had a loud and happy smell that could not be ignored. Even as kids we understood something of that magic. It was as if the coffee had hands, which it would put around our faces and try to draw us to its chest. They were strong hands and would not give up. Even after the coffee was made, the hands came up out of it as steam, and they still tried to wave us over.

But no, my mother said, no coffee for us, and that was that. She would send us outside then, to play in the garden with our small cups and saucers that we had made ourselves out of white clay. We liked playing best under the peach trees, but sometimes we ventured under the apricots and the mulberries.

There were some hills made of clay, and we used their funny dirt to make things. Usually it was red. Sometimes there was some white. We would mix it up with some water and make a *masa*, like for tortillas, and then we would roll it out and form things. We would let whatever we made bake in the sun, and this is how we made our toys, except for dolls. My mother, when she made our dolls instead of buying them, used old pieces of cloth or worn-out pillowcases, which she would fill with smaller rags and tie off at the most important points—a head, some arms. She would get the soot off the stove and paint a face on the dolls. They had big eyes sometimes. You took your chances. She would make hair out of yarn and whatever else was around. And she made them in all sizes, although I'm not sure this was on purpose.

I always wanted a doll with a china face, but they were too expensive. These years were a hard time in the world. The dolls my mother bought me, the only ones she could afford, were always made out of cardboard, but they could eat pretend food just as well as china dolls. I played a game we called "comadritas," or little mothers, with my sisters and sometimes a neighbor. We'd dress up with rags on our heads and we'd tie ourselves up with material or old drapes so that it looked like we were wearing long dresses. People wore long dresses and head coverings then, and not just in church.

We'd decide where each of us lived in the garden, and each one of us had our own tea set and table with chairs. We'd invite each other over, very grown-up. Then we would wait for someone to visit, and it was always a surprise. Someone would knock, and we'd say, "Who is it? Oh, *comadrita*, it's you. Come right in."

"Oh, thank you, *comadrita*."

"Not at all, *comadrita*. Would you care for some coffee?"

"Oh, *comadrita*, I really can't; my husband will be home any moment."

"Oh, just a cup, *comadrita*."

"Well, okay, *comadrita*, just a cup."

All our games had rules like that, and they all had songs to help us remember, but all the words and ways to act were from the grown-up world. We were making fun of them but practicing to be grown-ups as well. There were so many games, but I remember them all. The *pobrecita huerfanita*, the poor orphan game, and *bebeleche*, which is called hopscotch now. And the *pájara pinta*.

In the *pájara pinta*, someone would be in the middle of the circle, with eyes covered. We would sing a song like in the other game, but the person in the middle would then touch someone in the circle without knowing who it was. She would kneel and ask if this were her true love.

"Would you give me your left hand, would you give me your right hand, would you give me a kiss?"

THAT'S WHAT we would do on regular days, but today was different. On regular days my mother would do her chores and my father would go to work. He worked as much on the American side of the border as the Mexican side, which is where we lived. He was a carpenter, though sometimes he sold houses. One could do that in those days. His most regular employer was Mr. Contreras's funeral home. It was on his days off that my father sold homes.

We didn't live on a regular street. We lived at the top of one of the many hills, and there were only trails leading up to the houses. Our address was Calle del Cerro No. 10, which was really the name of the trail that went through the little canyon between hills. That kind of place is called a *callejón*. The house was pink and made of adobe and brick, with two large rooms and a kitchen, all covered by a roof made of tin with laminate. The house was very warm in the winter, and we didn't use a heater. When it was hot, the house was fresh and cool. It was built right up against the side of the hill, right into it, with the hill being almost its fourth wall, and this helped. We weren't on top of the hill—we were part of the top of the hill.

It meant we could see everything, which was going to help us on this day. And not only could we see everything, we could smell everything as well. This wasn't as bad as it sounds. Every day at midafternoon, about three, my mother would make the coffee. On the days when we could afford it, she would send us to the bakery for fresh sweet bread, usually to the Norteña—there were two we could choose from in the neighborhood. There were bakeries all over in those days. The bread they baked was ready every day at 3:00 exactly, and we would wait for the smell, which was like a clock. Whether we had bought sweet breads or not, their smell told us when it was time for the afternoon coffee.

If my mother had a guest, even a neighbor, they would go

inside and drink the coffee, or sometimes Chinese tea. But they would never stand outside in those days. I had heard the grown-ups talking, that there was a revolution coming, a change of government. They talked in secret, which just meant that they were always talking in low tones.

The neighbors would gather and talk inside their houses all the time. This was all before it happened, what I'm going to tell you, and I didn't understand much of what they were saying. There were rumors, though, and as a child I was always curious. I always wanted to listen, even though what they said was mysterious and in big words. Maybe I wanted to listen just because it was mysterious. That's how I was. The talk was like a magnet to me.

Well, on this day, in the morning, my mother didn't let us play under the peach trees. We had been hearing airplanes flying all around and coming close to houses. At least we thought they were airplanes. That's what people were saying, but they made all the kids stay inside and so I never got to see any. But even from inside the house we could hear the people standing outside and saying things like, "Here come the Obregonistas," and, "We better do something."

They were all shouting as the morning went on, and then crying. We went out of the house too, finally, when my mother couldn't stop us, and I saw my father running toward us up the hill. It was almost noon but too early for him to be coming home for lunch. Because we were so high up, we could see people crossing the line to the American side. They had opened up the *garitas*, the guard stations, and seemed to be letting people go right through.

My father arrived scared. He said to my mother, "The hour is here, and they're going to kill everyone." My mother made us all go inside and get on top of the bed. I don't know why, but at least that way she would know where we were.

"Let's go, let's go to the other side," my father said.

But my mother was very calm. Quietly she said, "No. We're not going. If we're going to die, we're going to die together, and right here." I don't know what else they said to each other because by this time, we were all hiding under the sheets and pillows.

The noises of the airplanes got louder, and we began to hear explosions. There was noise everywhere. One of the neighbors yelled to everyone that they were bombs, but I didn't know what that meant. But I could hear the people in the *callejón*, which echoed everything up to us. I could hear as the whole street cried and moaned.

Between the stove and the wall, in the kitchen of our house, there was a little space, and that's where my mother put us. It was a very small space, and there were five of us. My parents put their arms against us and held us tight against the wall. I don't know how long the bombs and the noise lasted. It wasn't a day. It might just have been an hour or two hours when the noises finally started to go away. But that hour or two is bigger than almost any other day I can think of. It's bigger than some months.

My mother said finally, "They're gone."

My father said, "I'm going to look out the door." Everything was quiet, which was as loud now as the noise had been. "Yes, they're gone, there's nothing out there. *Se arrepintieron*," he said. They must have felt bad for what they had done, he figured, and given up. Who wouldn't? But he didn't really know.

WE WENT OUTSIDE and we could see the neighbors coming out, and the people farther down in town. The neighbors were all checking with each other—did anything happen to you? Were you afraid? I was. I hid. We didn't know what else to do.

There was some laughter, but it wasn't like other times. People seemed to shiver, and shake this feeling off like a dog throws off water. They didn't mean to do it, but I could see the way they suddenly moved.

After this, we heard that bombs had actually fallen. One dropped close to the house. The hole is there in the *callejón* to this day. They left it on purpose. An airplane also fell. The authorities did not have airplanes of their own, but they managed to shoot one down on Canal Street.

The pilot was alive, we heard, but we never knew what happened to him. And nobody else died either. Afterward, it was kind of funny, in that it all went off so badly. They had just been dropping bombs out of the airplanes, but they had to steer them as well, so they never could aim very well at anything. Things would be different today, I know, but that's how it was.

We don't know why they bombed the town. To this day, we don't know. That's how the Revolution was. That was the year President Obregón was assassinated, and the bombs may have had something to do with that, but we didn't know. Everyone just shook their heads a lot when they talked about it.

The funny thing is, the bombs did not end there. During World War II, the Japanese had a secret weapon. They had the idea of putting bombs on hot air balloons and letting them float across the Pacific to the United States. They were supposed to kill people when they blew up and start fires in the forests and cities and destroy buildings. Whatever a bomb could do.

People didn't really know very much about the wind yet. The Japanese had just discovered that the winds came in this direction, that they blew for over five thousand miles all the way from Japan to the United States. They had to make the balloons light enough to fly but strong enough to last. They used some kind of paper that came from mulberry trees, just like the ones we used to have around the house. Remember the peach and apricot trees, too?

Well, the plan didn't work very well, but they did do it, and the bombs did reach several places. But it was like the bombs they dropped from the airplanes when I was young—they couldn't aim these very well either, not over five thousand miles. And the thing is, one of them reached Nogales. It was on the American side, but, you know, it's still Nogales. But it was like the other bombs— nobody got hurt, and nothing much happened. They just found the balloon paper and some bomb things.

Nobody ever really believed they came all the way from Japan, but it turns out they did. The people who knew how to figure these things out figured it out, but nobody was supposed to talk about any of this, no matter which side of the border you were on. Nobody was supposed to let the Japanese think that their plan had worked. Of course, we heard all this a long time after the war was over. Even so, we still weren't supposed to say anything. I still feel funny talking about it.

So there we were, being bombed again. And it was just as silly and accidental. I say it was an accident because we never did anything to be bombed for. Not that anyone ever does, but we really didn't. It just seemed like a good idea to someone somewhere else. I don't know what it is about this place.

The second bomb didn't amount to much. But I was five years old when I heard those first bombs, and they were loud enough to last up to now, to the end of the century. If they meant to scare five-year-olds, then it worked, and very well. But I remember the coffee from that time too, and that must mean something.

What I Heard from the Bear

In the early thirties, people used to die differently. We were living in Nogales, and when somebody died—a neighbor on Calle del Cerro, where our house was, or maybe somebody on Buenos Aires Street on the next hill over—we would all come out of our houses. Somebody dying was a party for the children and meant a good smell in the air, even if everyone was crying. I was one of those children, and I remember death that way.

It was my father's death that I remember most of all, but I don't remember it as any different from any other. I'm sorry for this. The things around a death—even my own father's—they took a person by the nose and by the hand and by the ear, so that the heart had a hard time making its way through the crowd to take care of its own business. That came later, and lasted for years.

The moment of death always meant the smell of sweet bread and coffee, and sometimes rain, which in turn raised the passionate but quiet scent of the creosote in those hills. The moment had the sound of so much crying and people talking, but also of dishes constantly being moved in the kitchen. It had the taste of so much candy, so many little packets of *cajeta* and bars of fresh fudge and *cochito* cookies, sometimes washed down with *café con leche* or sometimes with rainwater. And a death, most of all, had the feel of starched clothing, which is what one always wore, starched clothing that never fit because it was kept in a drawer for just these occasions—even though one had always grown since then. But since it wasn't old or torn, it could not be thrown away—it was all this that death brought with it, the weight of so much, so much. The moment was always bigger than whoever died.

41

Even my father. I remember him, in some ways, as everyone who died in those years. Somewhere in the midst of all of them, somewhere in the crowd, I lost him.

IF SOMEONE died in the morning, this was very considerate, and the whole affair was easier on everybody. The neighbors had more time and would get everything ready for that night. People in those days had to be buried within twenty-four hours or else things happened. Everybody knew this.

At about three o'clock in the afternoon, after people had gone to pay a respectful visit to the funeral home for instructions on what to do with the body, though they already knew very well, they would go to the *mercado* to shop. Normally all the regular shopping was done in the morning, but for a funeral one had to shop no matter what the time and hope that there was still bread.

People then gathered at about four o'clock at the dead person's house. The funeral home was a show for The Public, but this next part of the day was for the neighborhood, which was very different from The Public. The neighborhood was more family than family, though nobody ever said it that way.

If there was money, they would have bought what was needed for making *menudo*. Since it took so many hours, there was always a little bit of a hurry to get the *menudo* meat cooking so that it would be ready for the evening. Different families brought the smaller things, the sugar, bags of fresh coffee, sweet bread, and whatever else might be popular that year, or else something that was a remembered favorite of the dead person.

My father liked sweet bean tamales, which were a children's dish and which he remembered from his own childhood, but they couldn't be made so fast, so nobody talked about them. Of course, not talking about them made their absence all the greater, leaving something unsaid about my father, unsaid and sad. My mother never made bean tamales again, and I did not taste them myself until many years later, when I made them myself for you.

The neighborhood would also make its exchange with the hills, with nature itself. Giving the person over to God and the ground meant something more than digging a hole. Stomachs had to be filled, of course, to account for the absence, but there was more. Things had to be readied on all accounts. They used to send the young girls into the hills to gather *romerillo* or *palmilla*, any of the plants that would break off in strands or small branches. Once they brought those branches, they were put outside or in the room where the body was. Filling the room with leaves and flowers was a way of helping the dead person take a first step, with the whole neighborhood there to help.

BY DARK, THE dead person's relatives would begin to arrive. The men would bring *aguardiente* or wine, sometimes tequila. They would also bring cinnamon and lemon to make hot drinks lasting and bitter enough to stand against the cold of the coming night, and the recognition that the dead person could have been anyone, including and especially themselves.

The funny thing about all these relatives—they were always the same people. We were related to everybody, and everybody was related to us. Nobody said it like that exactly, and many hours were spent at the kitchen table sorting out who was related to whom, and on which side, and so on, but the truth of it is, the whole thing was a big jumble. One way or another, whoever this dead person was, you were related.

The dead person would be laid out on a table covered with a white sheet. If it was a child, they would put flowers all around the body so that it looked like a photograph in a picture book from the last century, with so many petals for a frame. There were boxes now, coffins, but people would still sometimes wrap the body. Keeping the cold away was a habit that would not give up, even in this moment.

While the women were inside at the wake, praying the rosary around and around, the men would stand outside. People would take turns keeping guard next to the body through the hours of the night. The men started out, but they would get drunk, then drunker. Then they would start putting their arm around the dead person and striking themselves on their chests. But this noise didn't last long, and they would fall asleep even as they were shouting and in tears. By morning it was the women who stood next to the body. The children would guard too, in the beginning, standing like angels, but only until bedtime.

I stood there many times. I think I stood there for my father. I don't remember because I remember looking at him much more than away from him. The angels, when they stood, were always made to look away so that they would not get scared. I think I did both.

IF A CHILD had died, none of this happened. A child's death was always different. Sometimes families could not afford new or very nice clothing to bury their children in, but those who could would have someone make burial clothes out of voile gauze and lace. Underneath, the underwear would be what was called *piel de ceda* or *raso*, always white. Everything white.

If the family was poor, they would make a white crepe paper outfit, a dress or a small suit. Using the white crepe paper, they would decorate it with lace at the cuffs of the sleeves and pants. Sometimes they would get very small seasonal flowers. If it was November or December, for example, they would use small, yellow daisies, which they would sew to the clothing. If it was summer, they would use sweet peas, *chícharos,* or French lilies.

Always they would put a crown, either bought or handmade, on the child's head. It was a crown of fresh flowers, if they were available. There weren't many flowers in Nogales—it was in the *pedregal,* the high desert, which was rocky and grew only shrubs, where there were normally only zinnias and *cempasúchiles,* the kind of marigolds that smelled but were the traditional flower of the dead, and that the Indians used. But for the wreath, people in my neighborhood and around us preferred to use small roses, *clavellina,* and small daisies, always with *siempreviva.* If you looked hard enough in the hills and the *mercado,* you could find them. *Siempreviva* was a plant that never died. It never dried out and it could be found around Nogales, even in the desert parts. It would sprout a bud, and then a flower, and the flower never fell off.

I don't know what flowers they used for my father, or if maybe they even put a crown on his head, he was so much like a little boy, still always laughing and playing with everyone in the neighborhood. I just always remember the wreaths and the crowns. I would think for a moment that kids were luckier than grown-ups because they got the crowns, which I liked better, but then I would shake my head.

A DEATH WAS a death. Who in particular had died finally didn't matter. People would come anyway, lots of people, and there was always family. My mother didn't like to go to funerals, though. That's how she was, and through all of those years that's something I still remember. Her and funerals. I don't know how she got through my father's, much less her own many years later.

At about five o'clock, the girls of all the neighborhood families would form a circle to start braiding wreaths out of *palmilla* or *romero*—this rosemary always smelled good—or mountain pine. Then they would entwine the flowers into them. Some of these were so good, so pretty, the flowers so thick that you couldn't see the framework of the vines. When you picked them up, though, the flowers would keep falling off. They were very delicate, and that's why they didn't make big wreaths until later, when they thought of other ways to keep the flowers on.

It wasn't until later in the next decade that the men would make frames out of wire. People eventually got better at making these things and had their own tricks. They got bigger and fancier in the next decade and became almost a competition, though who would have said so.

At about six o'clock, praying the rosary really began. There was a rosary every hour. People would talk and eat in between. Some would sing litanies and sing prayers. Whenever anybody started to sing, the singing itself would make people stop what they were doing and listen. Singing is like that wherever it goes.

At about midnight, the men were pretty drunk. Those who were not guarding the body would stand outside, talking about everything, and sometimes they would start to fight. They always did this away from the dead person, though, out of respect.

WHEN THE time came to take the body to the church, the big, black *carroza* from the funeral home would come driving up as close as it could get, and everybody was ready with flowers and wreaths. People would follow this hearse, which drove very slowly, down to the church. They would never go in cars, only and always on foot. They would go to La Iglesia de la Purísima Concepción. There would be a mass. These were the longest kinds of masses I can remember, and the church was always hot.

When it was finished, everyone would follow the body out of the church and walk down to Calle Internacional. The cars would be there, and buses, to pick up all the people. From there they would go to the cemetery. There were several: the Rosario, the Nacional. Sometimes you went in the other direction to the Panteón de los Héroes. The dead, it seemed to me, had plenty of their own neighborhoods.

The cemeteries would be beautiful on that day, full of real and paper flowers, boughs and leaves, crowns and wreaths, and sometimes photographs. But if it rained, as it often did in those days, the cemetery itself seemed to wilt. The rain on all these flowers had its own smell, and it lingers to this day as the smell of a great sigh, the smell of the flowers wilting.

BUT IF SOMEONE died in the afternoon or the evening, people had to move fast. It was all double time and easier or harder on everybody because things moved so fast, depending on how you looked at it, or how well you knew the person who died. But you had to go out looking for flowers in the hills at night, and that was difficult no matter what.

The town took its deaths hard, and the grieving was loud, and seemed like people meant it even if they didn't know the person too well. The wreaths were from the century before, a tradition that people remembered. It was a way of sending off the dead with something that those who had gone before would understand and recognize. A wreath of flowers was a small thing to send a loved one off with, a small thing but sure. In the thirties, this certainty counted for something.

In those days, before all the things that would come—radio and television and newspapers printed every day—there were announcers, with whistles. This is how funerals were announced. The person who was hired would walk all over town and shout up the canyons with a loud voice. Some would dress as clowns and some as bears. They had beautiful and clear voices. One used to walk on stilts. They used funny sayings to tell their news, and each had his own following. If you paid them, they would announce anything.

YOU KNOW what I have been telling you. It was just in this way that my father died, and it's what I remember. But it's all mixed up. His was a morning death, though, which was like him. I remember that. Otherwise, it was not more or less than I've told you. It was like everybody's. Except for one thing.

The stories and half stories that he kept in his mouth. All of them. What was in his pockets and in his chest of drawers, in the bank, and in IOUs, all that was accounted for. But I don't know where his real things were put, or where they went. My mother said the stories he was always telling weren't true, but I think they were. He lived in a different world from my mother, and different things happened to him. He let me see that world sometimes, and I've never forgotten.

Once it was a regular day, and my father arrived at about six o'clock. He never went out after six and was always at home with us. He was helping to build the canal through town in those days. This was about 1929 or 1930. I remember it was at about that time because we always had to go to bed at seven. We were starting to get ready for bed when my father arrived, scared.

We were sitting on our bed when my father said, *"Vieja, vieja, Rosa, Rosa, they're taking all the Chinese. You should have seen, on railroad cars. I'm going to go back and see."*

"Don't go," she said, as much with her eyes as with her voice. She recognized trouble. "Stay."

"No, I'm going to go. And I'm going to take her."

He looked at me, and my heart got big in my chest. It was a funny and sudden feeling.

"And just what are you going to do?" asked my mother, already knowing there wasn't much he would say. "And with her along. What are you going to do?"

"There are a lot of people watching already," he said. "They're all out there." He raised his eyebrows, and that was enough.

I was ready. My father used to take me out in the afternoons when he could. He would wink at me, and I knew. I would go get my coat before he even asked my mother. My mother used to get mad and worry, but it was all right. He would find a place to drink coffee, and I would drink chocolate.

I was young, and I don't remember how I got to where everything was happening. But I remember being there, with my father at my side. I remember it was night, but early. It was cold, and with *nieblina*, that light fog that makes everything seem like a dream—not shiny so much as glowing. We were in the rail yard, and I remember the train's big front light was on, and that was all. Off to the side there were many *furgónes*—train cars, in the dark.

Off in the distance, there was a long line of Chinese, with soldiers directing them. The soldiers would spike them with their bayonets and made them get into the railcars.

We didn't stay longer than five minutes.

The next day, there was not one Chinese in all the stores of Nogales, starting with our own neighborhood. El Chino Panchito wasn't there, and already some strangers were opening up his store. They said the shop was sold to them, but everybody talked, for years. The neighborhood would have done something, something, but there hadn't been time.

My father heard that the authorities filled all the railcars they had but didn't have enough. The soldiers ran the last of the Chinese off, again using their bayonets to prod and rifles to shoot at their feet, but I don't know where they went. The soldiers made them run into the hills. My father said that some of these poor people could only save their children but were not allowed to carry anything else.

Chino Leo was saved. His family, who was not Chinese, hid him inside a big radio.

I don't know if what happened that night came out in the papers, and nobody ever really talked any more about this. Nobody knew what to say.

The Chinese had a lot of stores, but their signs were all changed.

I heard many years later that some of the Mexican women went back to China with their husbands, but they were treated as badly as the Chinese were treated here, and most of them died. A few of the women returned, and a few stayed. The children were all right. But none of it was happy. That's what I heard.

The Mexican women who did go to China and come back wore kimonos and slippers all the time afterward. And they were all so thin, you could see their bones.

THAT'S WHAT I remember about that night, my father, and his dying. It all mixes up. He was so thin, I could see his bones when he died, and he was wearing funny clothes, and it was something like a train that took him.

My mother paid the bear man to tell everybody, giving him enough money for our side of town, but she didn't need to. Everyone knew my father and knew when it happened. Still, she let the bear sing it out, and he sang this news as a song. She didn't like going to funerals, and she didn't know what else to do, how else to make my father stop and listen, if only for a moment and if only this once, so that she could say good-bye.

The bear's voice was clear and strong. My mother knew my father would never be able to ignore some new piece of news. And his funeral, it was a big party, just like I've said, and so he would have to stay for a while and see what was what. That's why my mother paid the bear, because of what she knew my father would do. I've said these funerals were like parties, because that's all I knew to call them when I was little. A man dressed up like a bear only made them seem more so.

Funerals were always parties for kids, but even so, I didn't like them. I never said I liked them.

I heard the news of my father's death from the bear as he shouted up the canyons that same afternoon. I could hear it, even through the window in my bedroom. It was the only story of the day, and so he took his time with it and even added a little as he went from street to street. That's just what my father would have done.

The news this dressed-up man shouted and then sang was a funny thing to hear, and could not be true because it came out of a bear. It was a funny thing, for a moment. The bear had always talked about other people, and when I first heard it, that's how I felt. The bear was talking about my father, who had died, but this was my other father, the one out there who was another person in the world, a man that other people knew, a man who became a song.

My real father, though, what did this have to do with him?

THREE

❧ The Other League of Nations ❧

The crazy people had a convention, people later said, and tried to laugh the story off. But it was true.

Without prior advertisement, there took place one day in this town a chance gathering of the left minded. It was a coincidental meeting of those who were famous in this town, prominent in their human loudness as the oblong fruit of retardation and cruelty, and of laughter. Everybody knew them. But nobody said so.

In this way they were ghosts, ghosts at very least in that nobody saw them. They had the curious meat of invisibility. And nobody noticed when they were gone, as they were never there to begin with. It is the trick of small towns.

Today, however, they were all here, recognizable as the single-walkers, those who owned the last four hours of the night. They were the bothersome ones who sometimes knocked on the door, loudly, as if to come home or to ask where lunch was, and who were then shushed away in no particular direction.

It was inevitable, then, after years of wandering, after this and that here and there, after having taken an interest in stray dogs and trash cans and store windows and glass, the crazy people of this town, as they were called, would all one day bump into each other at the same time and the same place.

And that is what happened on this day.

And because of their training of years, at this convention they were all speakers, all group leaders, all fully and duly authorized representatives charged with championing their one cause or another. No one here was a member of the audience. Certainly not Mr. Luder, as anyone could guess.

This was a convention of ideals and a dead squirrel in someone's pocket. It was a convention of ambitions and desires, and the unmistakably urgent hand motions that go with them. It was Doña Jesusita's convention on her unending topic of morality, but without a quorum on any of her points one way or the other. It was Mr. Louie's conference on the nature of accident, of circumstance.

Except for Tavo, who did not know one way or the other, no one wanted to be at a meeting, but by chance as will happen on summer days the meeting began anyway. First it was two of them bumping one into the other at the corner of Obregón Avenue and Villa Street. Then it was the addition and convergence of the rest, coming not to help but to take sides. It might have been a fight had anyone thought to use fists.

Some took sides against each other. Some took sides against whomever or whatever seemed appropriate to the moment as they saw it: God, the noises, the county commissioner's second wife, who was said to make the real decisions around his house. And a second wife, anyway—who had heard of such a scandal? Several of these crazy people were in complete agreement with the rest of the town, of course, on that outrage.

Added to all of this were the passing innocent bystanders, who simply wanted to get by along the sidewalk.

Someone might have described this meeting as not anything official, not a meeting at all. However, each person here readily enough had something to say, an immediate point to be made, and more importantly, a great answer to be shared. Though, in Mrs. Cano's case, the answer came in the form of tricks to be played and people around her now to play them on.

They had, each of them, been hurriedly coming to this place all their lives. They had known all their lives there was to be a convention but had never quite precisely known where it would be or when. So they were sorry for their tardiness, each of them said, and it was time at last to get on with their business.

Mrs. Cano simply made an extended obscene sound.

Each person had an extensive list of important things, if not on paper, then in mind. Conventions are always summed up the same way, that there is never enough time, that just when the good things start to happen, it is time to leave.

But not so here. In that each of them spoke simultaneously, in that each of their ideas was of a world order, in that no one wasted time with the habit of listening: this was the brilliant meeting, and cause for all of them to leave happy.

Everything got said, everything got dealt with, everything, including the matter of the dead squirrel, which, it was reported, spoke aloud, proclaiming itself to be a certain Mrs. Cano from San Luis Potosí. Though as anyone could see she was a squirrel now, she had originally come to this town as a woman looking to visit her cousin. That was what she said.

This might of course have been a joke.

THIS SINGULAR meeting was so efficient it did not consume more than twenty minutes, the time it took for the delegates to pass through each other on the way to where they were each originally going on that day. But they were of many crooked walks and faulty postures, and had so many objects protruding from their various pockets and orifices, which they held and protected at all costs and against all odds—with the resulting falls to the ground—that for them to pass by each other took a little time.

But a twenty-minute meeting, this was a triumph. It held something for those who met, and something for those who saw them meeting. This was a meeting that had something for everybody.

So although the newspapers said very little about this first part of the afternoon, the assembly could not be described as a simple stroll upon which several people met each other by coincidence—it was not exactly this. It might have been just such a thing for other people, but not this time, not here. This was official business.

That was a phrase someone in fact used: "We are here on official business." There followed applause, but it was for a small trick Mrs. Cano—the deceased squirrel—was playing on the widow Sandoval, concerning a pointedly nasty showing of the teeth through which was being forced some bluish spume, some kind of liquid no one had ever seen before. They had suspected the existence of this liquid in life, of course, but to see it—well, that was the reason for applause.

But official business, or *very* official business, someone said, which was it?

Mrs. Cano again made an extended obscene noise.

Someone else said, No business was already too much business. The assembled adjudged this reasonable, in the same manner that too much business is no business, and so they felt exhausted, all this talk about business. It was time now to relax.

"After not doing so much," they said; "After not doing very much," Mr. Luder, who was German and knew these things, corrected, as was his custom. Whichever was correct, the conversation thereby and with its loudness put an emphasis on both "so much" and "very much," which convinced even the holdouts that something exhausting had in fact taken place, both so much and very much together adding up to a great deal.

But wait, someone said. If, as was being emphasized now, their work here could be characterized boldly as either "so much," in Mrs. Martínez's words, or as "very much," according to Mr. Luder's corrective, should they not then be paid? Something for their time? Had they not in fact heard this incentive all their lives—that if they did either so much or very much work, there would be some reward; had they not all heard that? Some money, preferably?

BUT OF COURSE no one listened, and so they did not get rich that day. And while the notion of exhaustion was a strong case, no one heard that, either, and so exhaustion was what they kept with them. But no one listened to someone saying that no one heard, so everybody left the convention happy, glad to have had the opportunity at last to be given a voice in the world.

This was particularly true of Mrs. Cano, who after that would not leave her owner, Mr. Louie, in peace. A happy squirrel, he would say to anyone who would listen, is too much. She was a dead squirrel, but a happy squirrel, now that she had made her contribution to the assembled.

So Mr. Louie later murdered Mrs. Cano again, and the neighborhood children put him on trial, showing a lack of mercy only children have. He was said to have murdered her in cold blood, though as there was no blood in the dead squirrel to speak of, the issue of this fine point took up the whole of the trial.

After the deliberations of the jury, who also ate some very fine cookies without offering him even one, he was sentenced to carry the body of Mrs. Cano around with him forevermore, a verdict which he accepted though it brought tears to his large face.

The tears were from laughter, but he could not show it. The trick after all was on them, he thought. These poor children. How could they have known? That is the way it used to be, in the good old days before Mrs. Cano ever spoke a word. That was when he had been happy instead of her.

He had fooled these children by letting them think they were the masters of everything after all. How could they have known they were sentencing him to a happy life once more? *Children*, he would say thereafter on the sly to passersby, *ha, they're not so smart.*

And the passersby, they would agree, and more often than not give him a wink, so that he began to think he was perhaps onto something bigger than the moment: an underground, a cabal of people who knew what he knew, that in fact children were not so smart as they looked. It made his head hum. People would come to him sooner or later. They would see he was dependable and that he had seen the truth finally. He would be given the secret instruction for which he had been waiting so long.

He wore the body of Mrs. Cano as a necklace, or, better said, as a scapular, since he touched it so much in concert with his prayers. He would be patient.

MR. LOUIE would be patient because he understood patience, unlike Tavo, the boy who understood nothing, or everything—but nothing in between. Tavo had found his way to this conference the way he had found his way everywhere else. By walking.

Tavo was not so much of anything or anybody, patient or impatient, just a little bit less all the time, and asking only for simple things, with simple gestures. Tavo, Tavito, they would call him, Gustavo, and Gustavito, and the kids and some of the grown-ups would gesture back at him, not always kindly. He was born to a good family, of a high social class, but out of wedlock, and so his name was therefore unspeakable and he was invisible because no one could see him. He was taken to, or rather, simply left at the orphanage, and there he grew up.

In 1940 he was forty years old, and this gave him some cause for small celebration. That he thereafter was as old as the year was always a source of renewed amazement, a charm for his life that he wore with an obvious pride, always smiling even when he was not.

The oddness of his circumstance and of that smiling was, however, that he never grew to be more than the moment of his being left at the orphanage: he stayed a baby, with a baby face and a baby body, bigger and more proportionate as he grew, but a baby's body nonetheless. And his smile was like a baby's, and his words. And as he saw people in the street, first to the ladies, he would say, "*ma,*" or "*amá,*" because he knew them to be his mother. "*Amá,*" he would say, "I'm hungry." And to the men, if he felt comfortable, he would say, "*Pa,*" and then "*Apá.*"

He would put out his hand and show them, I'm hungry here, taking his hand from the air and putting it first to his mouth and then to his stomach. And someone always was his mother, and his father. Though nobody would admit to this for fear of some greater obligation, by circumstance and by turns, by coincidence

and perhaps even by virtue of the occasional prayers on his be-
half, someone always secretly saved something for him, some bit
of food, a nicer shirt perhaps.

Sometimes he would move in for a day, and the family would
bathe him and change him, and he would find his way of apolo-
gizing for having stayed out in the world so long without coming
home. One day and for thereafter, the family of Mr. Jesús Cano
took him at his word, or his kind of word, and they shushed him
and kept him, and told him not to go.

Tavo followed him at first because he wanted to tell Mr. Cano
about Mrs. Cano the dead squirrel; did he know her? But Tavo
could not get the words and the story straight, and so he simply
followed Mr. Cano anyway, hoping that one day he would be able
to explain. It gave him great reason to stay.

Mr. Cano made him a small house of wood in back, by the far
corner of the yard, and each week made the house a little better.
Tavo stayed there, until for other reasons Mr. Cano became mayor
of the town. It was said that Mr. Cano became mayor sideways
because Tavo so often got lost. And every time he did, Mr. Cano
would go out and find him.

In that way Mr. Cano met everybody, as they never failed to
help him find Tavo because they did not want the burden of Tavo
on his own again. Perhaps, someone said, and at just the right
time, a man should be made mayor for just such a thing.

Though he normally could be found, after some time, lying on
a rooftop or wandering in an alley, one time Tavo lost himself too
well. Neither Mr. Cano nor the town could find him. He reported
Tavo missing to the authorities and even offered a reward for
word of his whereabouts, so much had he come to care for Tavo, so
much like a family member had he become. And a reward was
not too much for a son, and even less so for a baby.

After some sad months he got word that Tavo had been ap-
prehended and taken to Hermosillo or Nogales by one of the
social squads, which in those days were in charge of rounding up
the crazy people. These people were full of the contagion, it was

said, but of what they were contagious no one could be certain. Still, no one was sorry. All they knew was to wash their hands well afterward, for a week or two.

It was the one word—*crazy*—in their lifetimes that they later saw fall to the ground like a china teacup and break into a thousand pieces, each with its own name, diabetes, cancer, innocence, and the rest. But in these days they only had the one word, and anyone who was suspect had to be taken away quickly.

Sometimes in a neighborhood where someone like this had wandered, one could smell the gasoline and later hear the hundreds of buckets full of water being spilled into basins all at the same time before dinner, and then so much scrubbing that a washboard music filled the air, a music that said *go away* and *do not come here*. It was a music that found its way into all the work of the musicians in those days, a music that would not go away, just get fancier.

The two choices that the squad collecting these people had were to take them either to the special green hospital or to jail. But Tavo was not in the hospital, as Mr. Cano had looked for him several times there. Instead he had been taken to the jail, where people get lost, and at first he could not find him there, either.

But he was after all a prisoner there. When Mr. Cano found him after hearing the full story, which was all mixed up, Tavo could only say *"Apá,"* and could only cry. Mr. Cano also could only cry, and they put their arms around each other.

Tavo later died officially in the small house made, now, of wood and of golden-colored things.

Afterward Mr. Cano did not come out very much and did not keep up with anyone in particular outside his family. A man like that, people said, should truly be mayor, not thinking one way or another about anything, a fair man, without preconceived ideas, without emotions on the issues of the day. An impartial man.

But of course they knew what they were saying. How now, as the town itself was growing older, sadness increasingly ruled their lives. A sad mayor was something they understood, something they knew how to vote for. Sadness like his was a pleasure, only in that it was an old and more intimate friend.

It is sadness people vote for, not happiness, which always wears a new hat and is always ready to move on. No one was opposed to a new hat, certainly, and generally people even liked new hats; like the circus, however, they just never lasted, and there was always the worry, what if some mud should splash onto its brim from a car or some unmannered bird go by? With happiness there always comes worry.

THAT'S WHAT Mr. Louie kept trying to say. This damn squirrel Mrs. Cano, she's too damned happy. Doesn't anybody see that there's something wrong with this?

The *loca* Chuy did not think so. She petted Mrs. Cano and said, *Call me Jesusita. But mind you, call me Doña Jesusita, or else people will get mad.* And then she smiled.

No one called her Doña Jesusita except the priest, who was out of a job anyway with all the churches being closed down these days by the government. So who listened? Everybody else called her the crazy woman, the *loca* Chuy.

From the thirties on she made her place. No one took her because they could not catch her. She had a new cardboard or tin or dog-blanket house every night and the new morning for a house every day. And since she asked nothing of anyone, they stopped trying to catch her, even though they could have, now and again, as she grew older.

She was alone but talked enough to keep herself company, so that she did not notice that she was alone. Nobody knew how she made it through the night. Sometimes there was a terrible snow in those days, a freezing and a rain, a wind stronger than a man, with a shout loud enough to fill the space in between the hills of this town. Sometimes she would be in the *mercado*, sometimes in the streets, but never in the same place at the same time, as if she understood her responsibility as equal to the lawyer who was always in his office by eight o'clock in the morning, never once late in his nineteen years of practice.

One day, news would come that the *loca* Chuy had become pregnant, but by whom no one could say. The *loca* Chuy said over and over she was made pregnant by all the women of this town, and that's all she could say about it. Perhaps it was because she had a little girl that she said that, perhaps it was something else.

As her stomach grew, she began to laugh and could not help but show it to everyone as was her manner. In earlier days, the boys would say to her that they had heard she was not wearing any panties. *Liars*, she would say, and lift her dress to show them. *Yes, I do*, she would say, *yes*.

But it was work, as under her dress she would wear slips and other skirts and sometimes loose rolls of thick, colorful material, no matter how hot the day. Lifting them all was an effort. And when she was done with the lifting, they would laugh and she would look down, because in fact she was never wearing any, and she would laugh too and lift her shoulders in an *oh, well.* When she was much younger, she had forgotten one day to put any on, and that was enough for the rest of her life. She remembered and forgot things in that way, always for the rest of her life.

She would do it anywhere, lifting her skirts, as she would not tolerate being called a liar. Somewhere in her life she had learned it was not nice to be called a liar, and also that it was good to be nice, and so she never failed her lessons.

Part of the joke for the people who asked her, however, was that often, in combination with the heat of the day, the weight of her skirts was so much that they would pull themselves down. They would droop sometimes all the way to her upper thighs before she would notice, and with a casual and distracted motion pull them back up. The work of going under them instead of lowering them was the thing, now, as what was to be seen there was already familiar to everyone.

But showing her stomach was laughter to her as well, and she liked doing it. But that stomach finally made her too heavy, and she could not run away very well. She would be caught, finally, and taken to the Madre Conchita, which was the name of the house for innocents. Her daughter would have a long life, beautiful but with a serious disposition from the orphanage, and a secret beard like a man, which she had to shave very early every morning, and again in the afternoon as everyone slept.

She would grow up without her mother, about whom no one would hear anything more.

THE LAST man standing presently in the group had not heard about the *loca* Chuy one way or the other, so seeing her did not matter to him.

In making his way through them all, he found Mrs. Cano suddenly in his face, and when he began to say something, Mr. Louie smiled and said he hoped that what the man was about to say to Mrs. Cano would be bad.

But Mr. Luder shushed the man before he could say anything to Mrs. Cano. You would not be so quickly irritated, Mr. Luder said, if she were your wife, would you? Mr. Louie made a noise of disgust with his mouth and his fingers. Some wife, he said.

This last man, Mr. Calderón, had not thought himself part of this league, not one bit. He had simply been crossing the street on his way to the butcher's, not knowing that the butcher himself had already ceased functioning as a butcher, his profession pushing him the step too tender; that the butcher was in fact, as they would later say, crazy; and that his state of being was contagious, as evidenced by what happened next.

It was as if the whole town had caught it, the whole town and the whole half of the century, as someone would later say. And then someone else would imitate the late Mrs. Cano, and make an extended obscene sound.

Mr. Calderón was to enter the store, perfectly at ease with his charge of two pork chops for the evening meal. But after his request, and a subsequent discussion with the butcher, a discussion in yellow and in purple, as it was later said, and after seeing a magnificent collection of clocks on the walls instead of cow-sectioning charts and white paper rolls, Mr. Calderón would leave the store through the window, so that his own face, his own body, would mirror with bruises and with blood the yellow and the purple of their talk, some truth resident in being, by actions, the sum of one's spoken words.

It had been a discussion first of the eating of meats, then more generally on life itself, then of the clocks, the texture of the fine old woods, the delicate sounds of the movements, and the voices, almost caught in a moment of surprise and yet still able to be calm on the half hour, and then the full and growing conversation of the hours.

In the morning, the butcher said, there was little talk by his clocks after waking, but then more and more into the morning, with full directions for lunch and a discussion of one anecdote or another at noon, with a full twelve moments of voice. Then the sleep after lunch, until in the late evening and after supper there was talk again, into the hours, until midnight, the sometimes heated, sometimes loving twelve strokes of conversation again, and then sleep.

That was why, the butcher would say to him, many times now he could not leave his store until so late, for fear and for love he would miss something.

Mr. Calderón would nod in understanding, and it would not be a simple social gesture, not this time. He would understand. And after saying good-bye, he would leave—because the world for him had changed even more than the butcher would know.

It was perhaps nothing the butcher had done. Perhaps it was. Perhaps he had caught this something as a germ, a germ that would turn out to be simply an odd turn of phrase, a curious mispronunciation, or an accidental juxtaposition of words not heard before. That. The kind of thing that changes a life. The school of the Moment.

Mr. Calderón would walk through the glass of the shop's window of his own volition, and it would break as a glass jar thrown against a wall, breaking into so many excited pieces, so that the whole group assembled in front of the store would be covered with a hundred stars each.

After doing so Mr. Calderón would be led to the front of this convention, the front more or less, as much the front of this group as a front was possible.

Though they would all turn left and right, up and down, not looking at him, he would on that day become by acclamation, if only his own, and by virtue of his singular act of the last five minutes, the visible red emperor of everything and everyone.

At that moment, the butcher stopped being the butcher, the town stopped being the town: perhaps forever, perhaps only for the moment. It did not now matter which. They were all suddenly caught in the place with Tavo, everything and nothing, but not in between. It was the place of every nothing.

Like all these other assembled kings and presidents, field masters and divine beasts of the fire, Mr. Calderón in his exultation would then in that moment wear his own squirrel, which was his pants, over his face and head, and his crown, which was the last piece of window—still shined, still clear—would hang pinned by its points like a burr to his skin.

❧ Don Gustavo, ❦
Who Had a Hand for an Ear

One sees the world differently from the rooftops of a town. The people are a little smaller, with bigger heads and smaller feet. One looks down onto the tops of trees and bushes. A small horse is like a large dog, a dog is like an awkward cat, and a white cat is like a comet or a falling star, only sideways, along the darkness of the street.

On a rooftop the air is colder, and the sound of people's talking is indistinct, no different from the turning handle on a meat grinder or the loading and unloading of boxes from a delivery truck. A woman's sharp laugh is a bicycle bell, but from up on the rooftop you yourself had better not laugh.

It might be all right if one has business on the roof—if one is, say, installing a new cooler or fixing tiles. Then a laugh heard by the woman on the street seems like no more noise than a mosquito flying by. But if your business is something else, the mosquito bites, and the lady points and yells. And there's never a very good explanation.

After the yell, dogs begin to help, feeling called by the loud sound of alarm. Then—I've heard this—two dogs begin to bark, in a cooperative tandem, one dog barking as the other takes a breath so that the sound is constant, a full and muscular push of sound rather than a momentary jerk. This full sound, together with the person yelling, brings everybody outside, and all the lights go on.

It is like being startled out of bed. However, instead of it being only you suddenly awakened, it's as if the whole town is you. You getting up and rubbing your eyes is everybody getting up and rubbing their eyes. And however you feel in reaction to this disturbance is how everybody else feels, all of it underlined by the dogs who have now been roused, with the added exclamation points of the babies who start to cry.

This is all if a person is up to no good. Otherwise being on the rooftop is quiet, and far away. It is a place better than sleep. Being so high, you get to fly as you would in a dream. The world wavers and music is heard in the distance, but you don't have to wake up from this place.

I like it. I get on the roof to get on the roof. Sometimes the ground is simply not enough to stand on. I have no business being on the roof—except that is where I have spent much of my life— but I have no particular business on the ground, either. I will someday have reason to have business under the ground, but that day is not here, and climbing high onto the roof is as far from that place and that day as possible. That may be as good an explanation as any. It is as far away from death as I can get.

But who would understand? Being on the roof is trouble if you have no reason to be there. It's that simple. That's why something had to be done about me.

It's always the same. Somebody sees a figure on the roof and shouts, "Hey, you up there! What do you think you're doing?"

Someone else stops and says, "Come down. Do you hear us?"

And another says, "Someone call the police. Quick!"

But then they see who it is—that it's me—and everything quiets down.

"Oh, it's you, Don Gustavo," they say. "Okay, then. Sorry. But be careful."

I wave back, nodding my head to say yes, that I will be careful.

Things weren't always so easy. When I was young, not yet a teenager, I got into trouble all the time for climbing up here. There's no crime in scaling your own roof, of course, but that was never enough for me. I got up on anybody's roof that I could. When I became stronger, I began the habit that I have today of carrying a ladder late in the afternoon, in preparation.

At first I was trouble for everybody, but then, when I didn't change, things themselves changed. The magistrate, who was by this time like a father to me, finally decided that climbing on the roof should be my job in this town. At the town council meeting he proposed that I be given the job of constable, even at that young age, seeing as how I was already doing the work of looking out over the town. Even though it was the job of honorary constable, there was a great deal of grumbling, as I recall. But the vote was unanimous.

Now, when I walk down the street with my ladder, it's easy enough. "Good afternoon, *señora*," I will say if I pass someone on the street.

"*Buenas tardes*, Don Gustavo," the person will say, very politely and without a second look at all.

"Ah, Doña Jesusita," I will say, if it's somebody I know. "How are you this afternoon?"

"Fine. And good afternoon to you."

"How is your husband?"

"Much better. Thank you for asking. Who is the lucky one today?" she will ask, looking at the ladder.

"I don't know yet," I always say. Choosing a roof is never so easy. This is hard to explain to people, and so I let it go at that. The truth is, I must wait for the roof to choose me, and listen for when it calls me.

"Well, be careful," she will say.

"Of course." And with that I find my way.

THE WHOLE story is not as easy as I've made it sound. In the beginning, my climbing on these roofs was a problem for everybody who wanted to sleep, and for everybody as well who thought I was lost and who went out looking for where on earth I might be. But the dogs would spot me. They'd begin to bark, and everybody would get upset.

Darkness concealed me most of the time and gave me the gift of invisibility. I tried getting on the roof in the daytime, but it was a completely different affair. To begin with, a roof is preoccupied in the daylight. It is completely still and quiet, and a little hot to touch. Perhaps its energy is in the tension of holding the sun, which, when I have held a hot plate in my hands for too long, I understand. Or perhaps it must act like a roof so that it can keep on being a roof and not become fodder for the fireplace. A roof that does anything out of the ordinary immediately calls attention to itself.

"I heard my roof make a funny noise last night," someone might say.

"Well, funny noises, they're just the start, aren't they? My cousin heard a noise in his roof last year, and it was little spiders. They were eating the house, filling in what they ate with spider webs and eggs."

"That sounds terrible."

"I would get my roof checked if I were you," says the second person. "And you might mention my cousin."

"Of course."

At night, on the roof, you might think I look at the stars. I do, of course. It's quiet in the sky, and naturally one is invited to look up. But the quiet ends with the look up. So many stars are loud to my eyes, and there is such a great roar I cannot look for long. The sound overwhelms me. So much clamor prevents the human ear from distinguishing any one sound in the world. And so, in truth, we ignore what we hear from the sky. We have no choice.

Looking down is easier, and it's what I do most of the time. A few voices, a cat and some dogs, a door closing—these I can understand. I know these things by their names, and they know me. The distance between where I am on the roof and where a person might be on the street is my kitchen table—it's at this distance, and between these two places, the street and the roof, that I talk to everyone, hear gossip, and listen for remedies when I've been bitten by an insect or cut by a pyracantha bush while climbing up my ladder.

Getting news is not always easy. I get regular news by talking to people, like anybody. But my ears have grown bigger through the years from so much listening, especially to what is being whispered. To hear what is whispered, I've got to cock my head sideways and let my ear lift up and reach out. I do this best with my left ear, which has grown to the size of a hand, though no one is unkind enough to say so. I have thought more than once that my ear might take flight, right off my head, as I strained to hear one thing or another.

But my ear tries hard, and I have heard many secrets this way. People use their hands to guard the words of their secrets, but they forget about words going up. It makes me think that if we ever figure out how to listen to stars, we will hear only secrets. We will learn, much to the stars' embarrassment, what Mr. Mars thinks of Mrs. Pluto.

The planets are not stars, I know. But since I learned where the planets were, I've studied them for a long time and can't say there's as much difference as people say. Of course, since I am looking at the sky and not in a book, I might be wrong. The truth is, though, no matter what anyone says, stars and planets look to me like a few more porch lights in the middle of a dark, fantastic city. It's the place where shadows go when their daylight work is done.

The dark I think is like that, so many shadows in every length and size they blend together and you can't tell them apart.

But the secrets are the story I want to tell you. And it's why they made me the constable of the town. One might think it has something to do with a great crime, but it doesn't. The police and the others like that take care of saving people from crimes. My story has nothing to do with anything so easy.

MY STORY is I saved the town from embarrassment, which is worse than a crime. The punishment for a crime is going to jail and that's that. The only jail for embarrassment, however, the only jail is to stay in the middle of everyone who knows what you've done. This is a place of narrowed eyes and quick glances, of seeing people speak to each other quietly behind their hands, which perhaps—if only briefly—point at you, and of people seeming not to see you. I like the invisibility myself, though not everybody does.

An embarrassed town, however, is too much. In such a situation everybody would point at everybody, everybody would talk about everybody, and so on. Nothing would get done. Whole days would pass without anyone knowing. I have seen how it is with one person and can only imagine the energy of a whole town turning against itself. There was the story of Señor Calderón, for example, and the black stockings. That story has energy to this day.

As for me, however, when I was young, I was always lost. I didn't get lost on purpose, and this worried everybody. I was on the roof, of course, but for a long time nobody thought to look there. I suppose bad things happened sometimes, but I don't remember them. I always started on a roof and ended up somewhere else. I don't know how to explain it, and it was embarrassing for everybody. They all kept losing me.

People wanted to point fingers of blame at each other and get mad, but they would imagine that perhaps I had been on their roof this time, and that's when they would quiet down. Who knew what I had seen? I never told anyone, though, and this is what kept me—and everybody else—from getting into trouble. It's also when people got in the habit of addressing me as "Don" Gustavo, though I was not yet a teenager.

My poor father rescued me every time, and I held on to him so tightly my chest is pushed in to this day, the spaces between my ribs still showing his fingers. That's where I keep him, in my chest, now that he is gone.

But one time, when I had gotten older and had a small mustache and wore a dark blue, good wool vest, and everybody thought that my getting lost was a thing of the past, again nobody could find me, and everybody thought I was dead. I heard them, at first, and I wanted to tell them it wasn't so, but that time something happened to me on the top of the roof. It felt like an elephant had stepped on me and continued stepping. I had always been the first to spot the circus train, and I would tell everybody in town, and it was always happy. This was not a circus year, however. Yet still I felt the elephant.

When I woke up, the pain from the elephant had gone, and I felt much better. I got up and looked for the circus, which must have come by surprise. I looked out at the town from the edge of the roof, and though everything seemed to be the same, the season had clearly changed.

There was mud on the main road, and the chinaberry trees were glistening. A woodsmoke smell permeated the air and made the town look like fog had descended. Some of the smoke may have been fog, and some smoke from fireplaces. Some was the breath of people out walking, their words steam.

I yelled to the people, but nobody heard me, which was all right. I realized I wasn't wearing a jacket, and someone would be sure to notice and shake their head. It was always better not to do things that made people react in such a way. I had no jacket, but I wasn't cold, so overall, things were okay.

I went to find my ladder so I could climb down and see what was what, but someone had moved it. I looked around, and my only choice for getting down from this particular roof was a pair of spindly eucalyptus trees. But they were tall and near enough to the roof—and this was not the first time I had descended this way. People often took my ladder, wondering who had put it against the roof since they could not see me at night. I was very quiet and never answered when they called, so dogs and babies didn't start themselves like motors.

I got down without much trouble except for the time it took and jumped over the fence of the backyard I was in. I walked to the street and saw it was either late at night or very early in the morning. The bar part of the Recreo restaurant was closing, though, and I heard everybody leaving. I recognized the voices and the good-natured complaining.

I walked up to two of the men as they began walking home,

but as I did some of the fog came between us in a small moment of wind, and the steam from their mouths covered their eyes. They were laughing and as a result looked like trains, sending up big, round chuffs of steam, made partly of air and partly of beer, and whiskey, and who knew what else. But this was a stiff kind of steam that moved slowly and was something to see.

Instead I walked toward Doña Jesusita, who lived near the center of town and who was at that moment emptying some trash. She was doing so with a little noise, and she was shushing her dog back into the door, saying that he would get a cold out here.

"Doña Jesusita," I said to her, "is that you?"

She did not answer, but she turned, and instead of going inside she stood in her doorway.

"It's me, Gustavo. Don't be afraid. It's just me."

Doña Jesusita looked around and pulled her shawl closer around her shoulders.

Her dog tried to come out again and started to bark at me.

"Don Gustavo, if that's you, go away!" she said, not looking at me directly but following the direction of the dog's bark.

I did not know what to say, and so I was quiet. The dog kept up its bark, and then like when I was younger another dog took up the work of filling in the quiet parts, the parts where Doña Jesusita's dog would take a breath. It was like the old days.

The lights of the town started to come on, and I heard a baby begin to cry. It looked different from the ground, and I felt trapped by the commotion. Still, Doña Jesusita's eyes did not meet mine.

"*Callate, gordo!*" she yelled at her dog. "Be quiet, you fatso dog!" With that she yanked at his neck.

"It's all Don Gustavo's fault. It's you out there, I know," she said, once again in my direction.

"Of course," I said to her, but she did not seem to hear.

There wasn't much more. Doña Jesusita got her dog inside and closed the door. "Abelardo," I could hear her saying inside to the dog, "Abelardo, be quiet now and eat your dinner." With that the dog quieted down and so did everything else. The lights started to go off, and the babies—there were two of them crying now—calmed themselves.

I did not know what else to do. I did what I could. I looked around for a ladder, but no luck. People no longer left them lying around these days, not after so many years of losing them to me. Fortunately I saw the permanent ladder at the side of the bar and was able to jump high enough to catch its bottom rung. With that I climbed up onto the roof and sat there. Again.

It's like that all the time these days. I don't seem able to catch anyone's attention, though they often say my name.

"It's Don Gustavo out there, I know it."

"That wind, it's not wind. You know who it is."

"Remember Gustavito?"

I hear it all. I am the biggest secret of this town, that I'm here but nobody can find me. I want to answer and try to when what I hear is about me, but something always gets in the way. A gust of wind comes up between me and whoever I am addressing, like tonight, or suddenly, on hot nights, a woman will flip open a straw Chinese hand fan and begin to move it quickly so that she seems to disappear. Always it is something. A cloud of smoke from the match of someone lighting a cigarette. And each time I wake it is always another season, which is disquieting to me and which I do not understand.

But I don't need a coat and am not cold. I like to hear people eating—it's when they talk the most—but I myself do not seem to be hungry so much anymore. I think being on top of the roofs feeds me and keeps me warm. And so many people calling my name is a comfort.

The Orange Woman, the Walnut Girl

I have always been guided first by the smell of the leaves. The cottonwood leaves in fall are full of moisture and sigh, while the big-ear leaves of the cactus suppose themselves indifferent to the world. They buy one good coat for life and stick with it stubbornly to the end. *Why not?* they say, shrugging their shoulders as if to suggest the spendthrift folly of anything else.

The privet leaves do not want to go away and try to hang on all year. They hear everything and want desperately to be friends with the world, very different from the mesquite, which goes about its workaday business, dropping leaves and growing more, always on schedule, with the added bonus of mesquite pods, so many of them and so happy in their bodies and their music but inexplicable given the attitude of that tree.

Be careful, then, not to put a mesquite next to a jacaranda, which is all delicate, fine lace and breeding, with its folded lavender handkerchief tips. If you shout at this tree or look at it cross-eyed, it will drop all its leaves and run. The leaves it can drop quickly, but running takes real work, and the rest of its life will be consumed by the effort. You'll watch it turn thin and stop eating, trying harder and harder and more and more to lift its feet from the mud.

The smell of all these leaves in their time has given me a way to remember my life. When the orange trees blossom, I know it. The smell is loud in my nose. And each season when the white buds start to awaken and I smell them, I think of where I was in other times. The moment is like a newspaper of myself—I am where I am, but I am all the places I have been as well, all in the moment I smell the orange blossoms, which, if a smell could be written, would be headlines.

SMELLING leaves, and watching their trees and plants, has taught me about people. Things are no different with people, except that they don't stand so still as trees, and they talk back to you. But they're not so different.

Still, in relation to the trees and bushes, I seem to be moving in fast motion. They're so slow, even in their season, even when the wind helps them to move and their leaves and branches look like the pumping arms of a person running. And I can't understand their voices very well, either. I know the cottonwoods and the pyracantha and all the rest are trying to say something to me, and they give me fruit and yellow and red and pink gifts and sticks and wood to build things with. I know this. But they are so slow to move and to speak that I get impatient sometimes, and move on.

It's the opposite with people. In relation to people, I seem to be moving in slow motion, and they all seem to be moving fast, even without the help of the wind. Sometimes they move so fast going by me that I feel a wind, and think maybe that the wind comes from so many people moving so fast all over town. In the midst of them I am so slow I feel like one of the orange trees.

I've tried to learn, though. I try to do things for people, like the plants do for me, but they don't understand. I try to give people things, things the trees have given me, but they don't know what it means. I try to make some of them slow down enough around me so that I can explain. These people, I have to try and catch one because they're all just a blur as they go by, even when I move my eyes around in my head trying to keep up with them.

Sometimes all I can do is sigh, or cover my head, or plead with them. But none of it works. They stand around me on some days, but what they're saying only sounds to me like laughter. When I can move away from them and go back to the things I know, to the trees and the creosote and the devil's claw, I try not to laugh back at the people. I don't think I like it when they talk to me with laughing.

And anyway, a laugh is never as good as an orange or a walnut.

Things people throw away are a lot like the trees—they don't move fast either. That's really how I learn about people, by looking at what they have left behind and what will sit still for me. That's how I spend time with everybody in this town. I see the pictures in magazines and on boxes, and that's how I've learned to do things.

There are sometimes good things to eat in there, in the places where people throw things, in the silver cans and the wooden cases. People sometimes forget about things. They forget parts of bread and small pieces of meat still on the bone, but I never know who anything belongs to, so I eat it because I don't think I will ever find them.

And I put on all the clothes I find, all the clothes people leave behind with the food. They keep me warm, which I need. Feeling warm is better than other ways to feel. I know.

People used to be slower, so I don't know what's happened. They used to be slower when I was smaller. I used to talk to some people, and they talked back to me. I remember that.

When the peach tree gets its blossoms, which is always before the apricot, I always remember, too, there was a woman, Doña Ventura, who often gave me a bath outside, in the yard behind her house. She drew the water from the pump and let it fall into a big, metal tub. She made me take off my clothes, but the cold of the water always made me feel like I needed to put my clothes back on. I remember too how Doña Ventura used to shush me, and talk to me, and tell me stories about all kinds of things. I could tell these were words just for me, and I listened very hard.

She told me a story about somebody like me who became a bird, which makes sense. I think that would be easier for me, and I hope it comes true. But I don't see any birds with clothes on, so I don't want it to happen yet. I need to know more about this before I let it happen. I don't want to be cold. I know this for certain.

One day Doña Ventura told me, "Chuy"—that's what she used to call me, ha! It's just what I was. *Chuy!* Everything else had a name, so why not me? And sometimes she called me "Doña Jesusita," just like the priest, which she said was my name too, but more, like saying an apple is red or green or yellow as well as saying it's an apple. That was okay too. Doña Chuy, just like her name, Doña Ventura. It was harder to say the longer name and not as much fun, but it said more, and some days you want to say more.

WHEN DOÑA Ventura gave me a bath she also washed my clothes, and so after my bath we had to wait for them to dry by a fire she made in the pit for the outside cooking. She put her arms around me sometimes to keep me from shivering and to keep me away from my clothes until they were ready. Sometimes I put them on wet, but she was right. I didn't like it.

"Chuy," she would say sometimes, "stay here. It won't be long." I liked it when she talked to me. And sometimes she would say, "Doña Jesusita, come back right this instant!" She would say this if I tried too hard to go over and put my clothes on. "And look at you, without any clothes on!" I would tell her that she was right, and that all I wanted was exactly what she wanted, which was to put my clothes on, wet or not. I just needed them on because that's how I needed them.

But she would hold me and keep me from going to them, no matter what. I didn't fight with her. I could have, but I didn't. These afternoons seemed to turn out well enough, and there were walls all around Doña Ventura's yard, just like her arms were around me. I usually hated walls and always tried to jump out of them, but here it was all right. Here it felt like I was surrounded by trees, like Doña Ventura herself was a tree.

One day Doña Ventura left me alone to wait for my clothes. She had to go inside to finish making soup, which she had not done before we started, and so she would have none to give me before I left. I liked her soup and so I sat there and didn't try to run. Not running meant I would stay, which she knew. I would stay there no matter what now, until the soup. That's how I am.

I huddled myself up. Without clothes and coming from the bath I was cold, even in the sunlight. Without my clothes it wasn't just the smell of the world that told me things, it was the world itself that I was made of. I could see it.

It made me think I don't know which world I belong to most. The trees and the plants all showed me what to do, more than people. I look like people, all right, and so I'm one of them—but I look like other things, too. On this afternoon I looked down and could see how my belly looks like a big orange, with the funny little thing that's like a hole but isn't. I think sometimes about squeezing an orange and getting its juice, and that is what happens to me. Sometimes, if I push myself, the same thing happens. I push myself and orange juice comes out of me.

Down where I make this water I look like grass, and so I use grass to wipe myself when everything comes out. I sit on the grass, and blend in, and it dries me. That's how grass can live by water.

And I think I am full of different-sized branches inside me. I might be a tree. I can feel them in my arms and my legs and can see them sometimes. And I can see the blue and the green and the red and the white strings and cords and vines that bind them all together. My hands and my feet are very complicated, and to make them must have taken a long time. I don't know who did this.

On my chest are two opened walnut shells, half on one side and half on the other. Sometimes I think they are small fists, clenched up, and sometimes they open up and sometimes they close tighter. That's when they're from the human world. But they're walnut shells more of the time, smooth and dark.

HE FIT ON me like a coat, but it left my back cold—he could tell. So he covered me around my back, too, by moving himself around. I wanted to be covered because of the bath. It always made me want to put my clothes on, but I wanted them dry. He was dry and as good as clothes. He would be fine until mine were dry.

He started to pull some other clothes from the line to wrap around me, a sheet and some pants for my head. He put them on me like a hat, wrapping them around my ears. They kept falling over my face, but they were warm from the sun and so I left them. I could feel the sun they held in them with my closed eyes.

He tried to climb over me as if I were a wall. But I could not help him. He tried to put his foot on me, as if my two hands were clasped like a horse's stirrup, but my hands were caught in my clothes and I couldn't. He put his foot there anyway, first on my thigh and then higher up. He found a place to stand somewhere inside me, but it hurt. I tried to tell him. It always hurts to lift someone like that. I wanted to tell him that it hurt and to stop, but my face was covered with my clothes, just like my hands. I tried to move but his foot was so firmly planted that I couldn't, not without making it hurt more. Then he stood harder and jumped, several times. I waited, but he was not gone. He must not have reached the wall, and instead, after a moment, he stood down, and gave up and was gone. He was so much in a hurry, just like everyone. I would have helped him if he had waited, but by the time I untangled myself there was no one.

WHEN DOÑA Ventura came out with a bowl of soup I tried to tell her what happened, but I didn't say it very well and she shushed me with a small sound and asked me what I was doing with the sheet. She gave me the soup and put the sheet back where it had been hanging next to my clothes. I wanted to say more, but I knew about being quiet.

"Calmate, m'ija," she said to me, and put her fingers against my mouth. So there was no more to say.

After that we sat together while I ate the soup. It had chicken in the broth, and leaves from the yerba buena plants that grew near the spigot of the water pump. The courtyard was full of light and the soup was warm, too. I held it in my hands. The fire that was drying my clothes made a small groan as the wood shifted, and some sparks jumped out onto the old bricks of the courtyard. Without the rest of the fire, they made themselves into smoke, which I could smell.

The arms of that smoke drew my nose to the smell of the jasmine on the vines, though it must have just started to smell because I had not noticed it until now. In the sunlight I could see little things floating in the air and could hear house finches and doves in all manner of flight and song. All the lines their wings made across the sky, and all the lines of the woodsmoke, and all the lines of the sounds they made, and all the smells in the air as well, all of it made a net. I felt as if I could leap up into the air and be caught midjump, and held suspended as if I were flying myself.

As if she could tell what I was thinking, Doña Ventura pointed at one of the house finches and said, "There you are. You're watching us."

I looked up at the bird and saw that it was true.

I had always felt like a tree running away, but just like the tree, my running took a long time. I wanted to be a bird instead.

AS WE SAT there and as I ate the soup, she looked down at the ground under me and said, "*Dios mío,* you've wet yourself." There was some water under me, under where I was sitting, water that had fallen from me somehow.

"This is too much, Chuy." With that she clicked her teeth and shook her head. She was not happy with me. I knew this sound, and it made me unhappy as well.

"Are you finished with the soup?" She asked me the question but did not have the time to wait for my answer. With that she took my bowl. I wanted some more, but she took the bowl to wash it in the water trough by the pump.

"Wetting yourself. Is that the thanks I get?" She dried the bowl with the apron she had on, then got my clothes from the line.

They were clean but had the smell of the woodsmoke from the fire that had dried them. It made me even hungrier, and made me remember things I had eaten. I put the clothes on, and then to leave I jumped over the wall instead of going through the gate. I knew Doña Ventura would shake her head and click her teeth again, so I did not turn around. I jumped onto the adobes, stood up on them, and then leapt into the arms of the trees, which lowered me gently to the ground on the other side of the wall.

FOUR

The Curtain of Trees

When José heard Rosa's older sister, Carmelita, at the door the following morning he said, "Here is the devil." It was not that he disliked her or that he did not get along with her. It was just that her being the devil was the truth.

"Look," said Carmelita, coming in with Amparo pulled behind her, "see what attention you paid to me—now look what I've brought back from that theater, look at this thing. . . . " She pushed Amparo forward.

"How did you get inside the building?" asked Rosa.

"With rocks, of course," said Carmelita, as if it were nothing but common sense. "Rocks against the door, until the old goat opened up, and then I went inside there and I got this one out and brought her and here she is. Look at her with her arms crossed! Are you just going to sit there as well with your arms folded? What is this, a family of monkeys? Is that all you have to say, folded arms?"

They all took a deep breath, Rosa and José and Amparo out of exasperation, Carmelita simply to fuel herself.

"Just leave her alone, Carmelita," said Rosa.

"Look, Carmen," said José, "it would be best, I think, if you left here. Every time you come, every single time, you get as mad at Rosa as you do at Amparo, as if she were a child as well."

"Don't you butt in here, Mr. Whoever-you-think-you-are," said Carmelita, "Mr. Eyelashes." She had always mentioned his eyelashes, as if they were what had caused all the mischief that was this marriage. "Don't you say anything in this . . . "

"I will say something." José stood. "Look, Rosa is my wife, and I want you to leave her in peace. And Amparo too. I will be the one to decide about these things."

"No sir. You both sit around just like this Amparo with your arms crossed because you don't know what to do. But she's not going to fool me like that, not me. She and this boy, well, they have to marry. That's it. And how I say. And immediately." Carmen was shaking, but not from weakness.

"Leave her alone, Carmelita," said Rosa again, calm through it all, looking at the floor. Amparo went into the next room. "Don't worry." Rosa spoke loud enough so that Amparo and Carmelita would both hear. "Amparo and I are going to talk. Then we'll go talk to the boy and see if he wants to get married. But we are going to talk to the boy first. The boy and his grandfather together."

"You have no reason to ask for permission; you don't need any authority from them," Carmelita said, in something half regular speech and half the sound of a motor. "The boy already did what he did. We don't have to wonder about that anymore, not the way I found them. So why are you going to ask anyone for anything, much less that crooked-standing old man?"

Then Carmelita began to talk about the boy's grandfather and couldn't stop—this part was all the sound of a motor. "This man," she said, "who should never have given life to anyone, and running his fancy-pants movie house of prostitution. . . . It's in those movies, you know. Don't think I haven't seen them. Don't think I don't know what's happening to Nogales, to the downtown. Don't think I don't know what kinds of ideas. . . . "

Amparo had hidden from everyone in the next room, and since wedding plans had been laid in these last five minutes, Rosa thought to look for Amparo. "How bad could it be," Rosa said to no one in particular, "going and talking to the boy and the old man?" But Amparo had found a way out of the house and was gone. It was an old skill of hers.

Nobody had seen or heard her. Rosa guessed that she had made a path over the top of their hill and down the other side rather than going down her street as was normal. This had been Amparo's secret, learning to be invisible. Rosa knew. She had never seen Amparo do this, but she knew. Rosa thought, if she herself had been smart enough to get away like this when she was young, she would have done it too.

This was not the first time. But because Amparo had gotten away again, when Rosa told Carmelita, Carmelita could not be smoothed. She danced, with fury. It lifted her off her legs and then dipped her a little. They were old and sure partners.

Rosa was no competition for Carmelita and was not asked to dance. Rosa's dance was the waltz, and like Amparo, it was her way to be invisible as well.

Rosa was quiet and took things to her chest, through to her heart, where she held on to them. Things did not enter her and then slide back out her mouth.

Neither did things slide out of Carmelita's mouth, not right away. Instead she had found a way of saving things, and, when they came out, they came out in a flood with a great many other things. When this happened, the sheer force of her words sometimes propelled her backward, the way she moved now. She could not be stopped. One day everyone in this house expected her to go right through a wall. More than one of the smaller children began to see her as something else, as full of the water snakes and the grinding flour mills and all the rest of the big things in the world.

From a small bedroom, these smaller children, Amparo's sisters, who had been pretending to sleep, all watched, with all the eyes they could summon. They watched Carmelita yell out her magician's unending and colorful, tied-handkerchief rope of words. The inside of Carmelita, they thought, was a very big place. Her small body was a trick.

CARMELITA, after making Amparo leave town, also made Rosa and José and their daughters want to move. They could never have said as much in words, but it was the truth. They could feel it. Carmelita was so big, there was not enough room for them all in Nogales. It took them a while to make the decision, but when they did, there was nothing else to say. Carmelita tried, but all the air from all her words only pushed them along.

Rosa and José chose Cajeme as a good place to move for many reasons, not the least of which was that they had other family there, Elena and Heráclio, and some cousins. *And* it wasn't too far. *And* they had heard so many things, so much good about the town, about how new it was *and* how strong. Elena and Heráclio kept saying *and* this *and* that until all the *and*s made a road, very wide and very easy.

Elena and Heráclio had moved to Cajeme because everyone else was in those days, and a few years later it was natural for Rosa and José and the rest of the Martínez family to come. Elena and Heráclio had gotten a new restaurant and hotel started, El Curaica, and they kept writing to Rosa and José.

"Join us," they would say in the letters, and the words were bold enough and inviting enough so as to sound like Elena and Heráclio were in the very same room with them. "Join us." Rosa and José had more kids by this time, so something had to be done. Carmelita could not baby-sit them all.

The restaurant was called El Curaica, which was a family name, but everyone called it the Sinaloense, because everybody knew Elena and Heráclio were originally from Sinaloa. Carmelita, however, did not come with everyone else, as she felt herself too much a stone wall or some other fixture of the town.

"Nogales is not that far from Cajeme," she said. "I'll come to visit."

Nobody doubted it. Carmelita did not let her family get out of her yard so easily.

THE TOWN was hot when Rosa and José and the kids arrived, but Elena and Heráclio were always like shade for them. Even without Carmelita to help, the world seemed all right here.

"Perhaps," they said with a laugh, a little nervously, "exactly because Carmelita is not here."

The town in those days had the look of a place straight out of a show in the theaters, out of one of those movies about the Old West in the United States. The town was all wood, all of it dry, with very wide streets. When it rained, one could not walk because the generous mud from the generous streets would ride up over shoes and onto ankles. The very large *mercado* was full of everything and had some things even beyond the everything anyone had seen up to then. There were six big streets of this sort, and around the town were fields, and the great gardens of Lamberto Diaz.

These six streets were, as was said, on the right side of the town. The railroad divided these streets, however, from what was on the other side, between the seed granaries and the flour mills. Beyond the station house of the railroad lay the Area to the Left, the Plano Oriente. That part of town needed no explanation, and when it was talked about, it was in whispers.

To the south was the immense row of trees known as "the curtain," the *cortina*, planted to protect the town from wind and the wheel-of-fortune cruelty of tornadoes. This was where the sweethearts went on Sundays or after going to one of the town's three social clubs, the Mutualista, for the townspeople; the Olímpico, for the middle class; and the Campestre, for those with some money.

In fact, the rich did not attend clubs at all, and everybody else tried to jump up a little: the middle class went to the Campestre more often than the Olímpico, and those with less money saved up and went to the Olímpico. That was the way to do it then, to save up and try to go to a little bit better place.

People walked that way, too, a little faster than they could. Everyone was in a hurry to get to the next place in those days.

But the true social club was Sundays along the curtain, with its winding tree line and pathways. Nobody walked quickly here, and the sides of the trees had a sheen from secret wear.

At first none of the children believed the stories of what the curtain was supposed to be for, how it was supposed to block the wind, as they had seen only couples there. And anyway, they didn't understand the need. They had seen what were called the water snakes and dust devils many times before in Nogales.

But soon they saw how so many water snakes came to this place and how sometimes two or three seemed to join. They could see then it was business. Between the couples and the tornadoes, that the trees were not either blown away or polished into rock was a miracle. Instead the trees had come to look like one of José's pieces of finely sanded furniture. The trunks of the trees had the feel of a nice living room, with end tables and chairs and the rest, very pleasant until the winds began.

The sky would cloud and the wind would start up. The first water snakes would start then, painting a blackness on the walls and the roof of the outside of this living room for as far as was possible to see. Then one could not see, but simply imagine, and closing one's eyes provided more light than keeping them open, and the world seemed upside down or inside out altogether. José and Rosa would put the children underneath the tables and beds and close the doors. Sometimes José would even tie his children to the bedposts and table legs.

Everything moved, the plates and the cups, and chickens would disappear suddenly or new ones would appear, startled and cocking their heads. Rosa would wet towels and put them on the heads of everyone under the tables, followed by her rewetting them from a bucket of water for as long as she could stand up.

José and Rosa both shouted, "Don't open your mouths, not for any reason, and close your eyes!"

With the water on their heads, the shouting of José and Rosa, the following of instructions, and the immense wind itself, everybody felt all right. There was no fear. None of the children cried. They were, after all, doing what was supposed to be done, so they were safe.

And from noise to nothing, just like that. José would say simply, "There."

They would all open their eyes, but they did not think they could see. So much dirt covered everything, they did not seem to be in their house.

Then they would start each time to build the house and themselves all over again, beginning with the palm fronds brought inside to scrape the mud and dirt off the tops of everything.

IN ITS FIRST years before the Revolution and for many years afterward, though people tried to change it, the town was known as Cajeme, named after the Indian Cajeme who fought on one of the many losing sides. The town kept the name at least until 1935, though some would say as late as 1938 or even the very early forties. But after that its revolutionary name took hold and stayed, more or less.

No matter what the name, everyone said Cajeme was the place to be in those days, and everything there was new. The Martínez family had moved there and lived in a good house on a wide street. Since José was a carpenter, he found plenty of work being, as they say, a handyman, fixing one thing or another. It was a good skill, as one thing or another always needed fixing, even though everything was new. That was the thing, he would say. An old piece of wood already knows what to do, but a new one must be told.

Rosa occasionally worked in the kitchens and was very good, for banquets or the popular picnic parties. She had learned this work in the restaurant and hotel El Sinaloense in Nogales, the first one, owned by her aunt Elena and uncle Heráclio when they still lived there. They had come to Nogales from Culiacán, and had given Rosa good work and extra training in exchange for her willingness to work more difficult hours.

Carmelita, who was unmarried and had no children at the time, agreed in those days to babysit for Rosa. While life in Nogales back then was not easy, with this help from Carmelita and Elena and Heráclio it was at least manageable. Who could argue with that?

In those days no fence divided the two Nogaleses, and everyone who was working on the railroad lines stayed at the Sinaloense and took meals on the patio. José worked across the border in the United States as an *enganchado*, which was like the *braceros*, but the *braceros* wore white and worked in the fields. They looked like hospital nuns praying in the mornings as they hunched over to stay warm in the pickup trucks going to work.

The *enganchados* worked on the railroad lines, laying down track all over the West, and they didn't look like nuns at all. José would tell Rosa about his work in the early days, about places like Stockton, Oakland, town by town, and about the Chinese, the Germans, the Irish who worked with him.

They worked with him, but not by him. "These other workers, they stay away from us," said José. Then he would shrug his shoulders.

"Maybe it's the way we talk, different, I think. Not like them." José said things like that, putting on the best face.

"The men stay in their groups," he went on. But the only real language he had from those days, the only way he could finally describe these places, was railroad tie by railroad tie. It was a little boring that way, and Rosa wanted to hear about Hollywood instead, so he did not talk about real days for very long.

EVERYTHING bright and new, however, had many meanings, and a move is still a move. To know why new towns start up and move forward, one must first look backward. For José and Rosa, though it seemed a good thing, the move from Nogales was still very difficult for them. More complicated. They were missing a daughter, after all. Because of this, the move was never fully a move.

Amparo's story was old now, but not to the Martínez family, not to Rosa. She could not stop telling it, if only to herself.

Amparo had apparently gone along with things, but not as much as everyone thought. When Carmelita had found her and dragged her home, she was fifteen. Because she was the eldest of Rosa and José's daughters, Amparo spent her time—as was customary—living with, and helping equally, both Carmelita and her parents. Often, Rosa thought Amparo to be with her aunt Carmelita, and Carmelita would think she had returned home to Rosa. Amparo's sisters were smaller and took no real notice one way or the other. All just as Amparo wished.

Amparo had met Pancho, a boy who had been orphaned and now lived with his grandfather, the manager of one of Nogales's two movie houses, the Cine Sonora. The boy and his grandfather lived in the few rooms next to the projection booth. This building was smaller than the other theater in town, the Cine Obregón, but equally nice. How Amparo met Pancho was unclear, even to the both of them, but she began going with him here and there with some regularity.

The first time Carmelita had caught them together was an afternoon very cold, and she had come out of nowhere, out of the blue and black and by surprise. Carmelita grabbed Amparo and took her, arriving at her sister Rosa's house furious, pushing and pulling Amparo in through the door.

"Look what I've brought you," screamed Carmelita at Rosa, and at José, and at the walls and the ceiling of the house. "Do you know this whore?" she continued, pointing at a shriveled Amparo and all the while hitting Amparo flat handed across the top of the head and shoulders.

Rosa had no idea what was going on. Amparo was supposed to be taking care of the other children, which she had done, in a manner. She had fed them all and then locked them inside the house as she went out.

Rosa had just come home when Carmelita burst in. The children had not had time to say anything to her.

"Look at her, just look at her," shouted Carmelita, repeating herself as if no one had heard her. Carmelita stood poised and could not be shushed, dramatic and with fists now in the air.

The other children began crying because who knew what this was, all this noise and hitting, and their sister there in the middle of it. They were a little glad at first that she got in trouble, but not like this.

Amparo was resigned and quiet, sitting through it all as if she were sitting in some other room and in some other time.

"Carmelita?" Rosa said. "What's the matter, what?" In that moment one could see Carmelita and how, as the oldest sister in the family, she was doing her job, doing her job exceedingly well, by being the mother to them all.

"But Carmelita," Rosa said again, "what?"

"This run-around girl, as if she lived in the Congera with all the whores in that precious Cajeme you're always talking about. Perhaps she did," Carmelita said, pointing at Amparo, "perhaps she did want to live there, in the Plano Oriente with the other women animals."

Carmelita poked Amparo with her pointing. She did not need to touch her for a dent to be made. "Is that all she can say for herself, nothing? Look at her, this shameless cat, up there inside the theater with who knows who. . . . "

"But Carmelita, how did you know?" asked Rosa.

"How would I not know," Carmelita said, "a thing so loud as this, how could you not hear it? What kind of question is that? Had you followed her as I did, this devil-child, and you her mother, not even knowing . . ."

"Carmelita, leave her—"

"No, no. No. Rosa, you are a weak woman, completely weak in these things. It's ridiculous. How can you say to me, leave her alone—"

Carmelita would not stop until finally Rosa had to say, "That's enough. Now leave her alone."

Rosa got up and stood physically between Carmelita and Amparo.

"Leave her alone, Carmelita," Rosa said again. "You are not her mother and cannot treat her like this."

"I have the right. She's been with me as well. This kind of thing, who can let it go on—"

"You don't have the right to treat her like this." Rosa's voice was low and measured. At that, Amparo got up and went into the next room. Rosa and Carmelita kept the hard and soft discussion going, the shouting and the whispering, the left and the right, the ceiling and the walls. The deciding about this Amparo.

"You just wait, she's just going to go away with him again. Perdition, I tell you, an engraved invitation to it, perdition, completely lost. I throw up my hands."

Rosa said the only thing she could. "Go away, please, Carmelita. Just go."

Carmelita did go, but she did not stop her side of the conversation, into the warm night breaking. She was still audible from the bottom of Jardín Street, and in the dusk made gestures explanatory and obscene backward with her hands and her arms.

After a while and a distance more, she looked like a train with steam coming out as she was still marching into the dimness of distance. In that near darkness, when Carmelita opened her mouth, one could see the red in there of the unmistakable coals and the fire of the engine.

ROSA STAYED quiet, and nobody moved. It felt like the moment after the passing of the water snakes, quiet like that, a remarkable quiet. Most of the smaller children could not hear the absence of noise, but Cuca could, the next youngest child after Amparo. Cuca could.

Rosa got up and called to Amparo, "You can go."

But Amparo was already gone from the house, having exited in some manner whose explanation didn't matter now. She was just gone.

"Cuca," said Rosa, "get ready. We are going for a walk." As the oldest child now regularly in the house, Cuca was her mother's companion in things. Her turn had come to learn the ways of the world in matters of the *mercado* and the afternoon visits for coffee and so on.

"We're going to wait for your father, and then we'll go."

When José came home at five o'clock, as he always did in these days, more as a formality than from any real finishing of a day's work, Rosa said to him, "We are going out to find Amparo."

She told him what had happened, and he said only, "Yes." He said it more with a slow nodding of his head.

Rosa and Cuca walked to the movie house and knocked on the front door, which was the only way they knew. The theater was closed, and so the knock was loud because there was no other noise. Nobody answered.

Rosa attempted a half-loud, half-whispered shout upward, "Amparo, Amparo," to see if she could get her, but Amparo did not come out.

Nobody answered the door, not even the old man, and so, thought Rosa with a small shaking of her head, they must be in there.

Rosa in that nodding remembered what she could remember about the old man and the boy: the grandfather was a little fat and had a distinct limp. He was sometimes in conversation between townspeople referred to by that limp, as people will do, as if that limp were his name. He was called El Cojito, but Rosa could not bring herself to think of him that way. And who knew, anyway, she thought, what might get passed on to a grandson.

The boy Pancho was light haired and light skinned, thin. He looked a little like Amparo herself and was her same age, near sixteen. That was all Rosa could remember.

As she could get nothing in response for her nodding or her knock or her half voice filled with manners, Rosa said to Cuca, "Let's go," and they went. On the way home Rosa cried but would not let Cuca see.

"It's nothing," she said. But Cuca thought it was something.

At home Rosa could not stop this crying, but she did it on the inside of herself now. Cuca could see it plainly, if the other children could not. Through the evening Cuca hugged her mother for what seemed like nothing and put a sweet roll in front of her at the table, and then coffee.

"Thank you," is all Rosa said at first. Then she added, because she saw Cuca needed to hear more, "I'm not hungry just now, but it looks nice."

The next morning Carmelita came again—this was the second time—again with Amparo, pinching and pushing her, both of them stumbling up the street and into the house. Carmelita was again shouting, but so much and so steady, the words came not only out of her mouth but out of her ears and her eyes as well, and she breathed through her hair.

José got angry, though he was a good man, good natured.

Carmelita knocked at the door with her words instead of her hand. "This shameless, this sleep-around, I threw rocks at the door and I got her out, this whore of a daughter of yours, this she-dog putting her behind up in the air, I say. . . . "

WHAT CARMELITA said normally counted for a great deal. She was, after all, people would say, the oldest in the family, which can explain a great deal in a small town. There had been five daughters in her family, and they had been orphaned by a father who had put—who can explain these things?—a toad in the *atole* they ate for breakfast one morning.

In turn, because she had felt it to be her duty, Carmelita—like her mother and father both had—ran each of her younger sisters off as they had fallen in love. Her parents had done it in just the way she was doing with Amparo. She was not using a toad, exactly. But it was close enough.

Now it was the turn of the granddaughters. "There will be only honorable women in this family," Carmelita would say. What she would not say was that she thought love was a dangerous thing.

She had learned to keep it out of her family so that the family would not be destroyed altogether. She saw love as being in some fashion her personal enemy, since it was taking all of her sisters away.

Love made babies, but it did not make marriages. Marriage was something else, something she could control. There was no honor in their leaving, she said to her sisters. Love, maybe, but not honor in going away, and she had cursed each of them in their leaving.

Even when her sisters did marry, she cursed them into their marriages, as she had not made the arrangements herself for them, and so she was sure they would fail. *"Putas,"* she called them, and worse. *"Putas,"* she said each time, as if she had suddenly found the word in her mouth and had to spit it out.

"This is what love is," she would say. "I love you so much, but see how you treat me!" Then she would yell at them again. "It's out of love," she would say, somewhere toward the end. "It's only out of love." That is what she felt for them.

Rosa had to stand by the side of each of her sisters and give them away. Then one of Rosa's sisters in turn had to stand by her when she married José, as Carmelita had made her views on José known as well. Rosa had not escaped. There was no escape.

Rosa's life with Carmelita thereafter had been one of convenience, but that in fact became again a kind of love between the two of them, a replenishment. It was something close enough to love, and strong sometimes. It held them together a little.

Amparo was older by several years than her sisters, and Rosa had lent her on occasion to Carmelita. Rosa did so to let Carmelita see that she was not leaving, and that her marriage would work. Amparo consequently over the years had felt comfortable living in both the house of her mother and the house of her aunt, as each seemed to want so much for her.

Amparo had lived in both places for so long, so many years, that the world seemed all right, until now. Carmelita had been quiet for a generation, but now Amparo was the first of the new ones to show an interest in love.

THIS KIND of thing, this fighting, this movement, this shouting so physically that it looked like a kind of dancing, became once more Carmelita's hobby, and she was good at it. Every eight days, without asking permission, Carmelita visited the family. There were no telephones for calling ahead. And what was the use of a letter?

When she was least expected, and whatever the place, there she would be. In the first years it seemed like luck, but not after a while. The Martínez family could count on her without fail. Sometimes to head her off, they would go to visit her first.

"Here we are," Rosa and José and the children would say, "we're here," as they visited her in her neighborhood, which was on the next hill.

"We're here so you don't have to trouble yourself and come over this week; we're here to visit you, Carmelita; how are you, how have you been. . . . "

"You're very welcome here, of course," she would say, "and now make yourself at home." She would make a fuss, which is to say she would say nice things very loudly, then she would prepare the big meal. Rosa would do the same, normally, when Carmelita came over. In the way these meals—which nobody wanted to eat—were predictable, so was the rest.

Once everyone was eating, Carmelita would begin, and one way or another a fight would start. A misplaced spoon, a dirty plate, any of these was enough to get things going. If there was a bread she would say to one of the girls, "Eat this bread."

"I don't want it," the child would say.

Then Carmelita would start with, "But you've got to eat it, your mother going back and forth like that to work, you better eat well here, you look like you're starving. . . . "

Carmelita would continue and could not stop, even after everyone would jump in and say it was not true, they ate well.

"Well, I don't believe you anyway, all of you so thin." She would then try to laugh, but there was not much behind the sound.

She had found her entry, and it was a new one each time.

José would keep quiet for the most part, but then he would say, "You know what you've got, Carmelita? A bitter taste in your mouth."

Carmelita would jump up, even if she seemed to remain seated, and start her railroad of words.

"You can't pass an hour without fighting," he would say, when he could find room in her talking. Then he would look at his hands and watch the hairs move on their backs as she aimed her mouth in his direction.

A point invariably arrived where Rosa would say, "I can't take this anymore, Carmelita."

"Well, don't come back, then. Who said anything anyway, the way you all come begging for food here, starving. I would certainly say nothing about that. Go, get out of here!"

That Carmelita had invited them with grandiose encouragement counted for little in the moment, though she would undoubtedly be prepared if they brought up such a detail. Any real discussion of who invited whom, and who should therefore be nice to whom, was hardly worth the trouble.

Rosa would follow with only what she could, what she felt—"I'm never going to come back to this house." She would cry, and take up the children's hands, and leave.

"That's right," José would say, "we don't ever have to come back here."

"Don't you dare come back; I don't want you around here anymore anyway," Carmelita would shout.

Rosa would cry for two and three days, because it was always the end, always just what Carmelita had said would happen, that the family would break and no one would come back to see her. And it was true, they would not.

José would say, "But don't cry, Rosa, you know how she is; she's like that with everybody."

During the times Rosa was feeling this way, she would speak to one or the other of her married sisters, asking if they too had gone to visit Carmelita. Each in turn would tell her story, which was the same as Rosa's.

Then the cycle started. If no one went to see Carmelita after the eight days, then there she would show up, asking to be forgiven, sorry for everything and did they not care about family, and was she not the one trying to make up? Couldn't they see this? Wasn't she here?

"No," Rosa would say, "not this time. It's too much."

"Rosa," Carmelita would then start, "sister, you must forgive me; I swear I will not do it again, I don't know what it was, sister."

Until Rosa would at least let her sit. After tears, and because of her diligence—her hardness—in making up as well as in argument, Carmelita would leave on reasonable terms. If there were enough time in that same day, she would go do the same at one of the other sisters' houses.

"I made up. For the children," Rosa would say to José, who never understood.

In later years Carmelita adopted a boy of her own and raised him. He suffered the same story, until one day he left and never came back. He was not her family after all, he said, and he could leave. Which he did.

For a while he became a pachuco in Los Angeles, but then he dressed regularly and got a job doing something or other, something nice, they all heard. He himself had a son, Carlos, Jr., but that is where everything came out.

The boy was not right, not exactly, and they called him Carlitos, because he was young, even when he was not. He loved to make gun sounds, and the army finally took him to Vietnam, where he said he wanted to shoot something.

By the end, however, he had found something inside himself that had been missing, and in his letters home he counted the days until his return. Before the sound of the land mine, he had counted three more days, and could barely believe it.

Before the boy, Carmelita had tried in one way or another to take each child for herself. After what she did to Amparo, she would do many other things. That was how much she loved them all. That's what she could not understand—why they did not understand.

PLUTARCO Elías Calles closed all the churches in the later days of the Revolution after all the troubles with the Cristeros. They had remained closed for a long time, but this was now toward the end, 1938, when Cuca was eight years old and ready to make her First Communion.

The opening of the church doors was especially in evidence as one was closer to the border at Nogales, which was a more daring place then. One could hear the deep sounds of the doors opening and closing there, even in the daytime—perhaps not with the ears, but with something.

Cuca could remember the beginning of all this, how in 1929 all the exiled generals passed through. She remembered how there were airplanes, and how it was said that the war would come here, but between whom was unclear. All that could be done in those days was to hide, and to put the children under tables.

Cuca was old enough to remember the war around the border from as far back as 1927 and 1928, the war between the two Nogaleses. She remembered it in waves, fast and slow both, and fast and slow and in waves is how she would later tell it.

She would remember a particular day, midday, when she did not go to school. She was told, "Go home, Cuca, and don't come out," and then airplanes passed overhead, which she wanted to go out and see. Real airplanes, of those she would be sure. She would see them, and they would look very big. They looked that way inside the house, inside in that place she dreamed them, bigger than the sky that held them. Cuca saw the airplanes very big because she could not see them. No matter how much she begged, and no matter how much noise, she was not allowed to go outside and stand under them the way she wanted.

At the end of all this, when Cuca was ready for her First Communion, the priest in Nogales on the Arizona side made it known that he would be at St. Joseph's Hospital for several days. The hospital, which had a small chapel, was then next to the border, and there was no real border fence yet. He had let slip the words "First Communion" and that he would be hearing confessions, or rather, as he said, *little* confessions.

Then he winked, and everyone understood.

Cuca, together with Carmelita's adopted boy, Carlos, was prepared, and had been schooled in the catechism secretly in different houses by those who knew the finer details. The two of them already knew the Our Father and the Hail Mary, but not the Act of Contrition, which was secret then.

The words stayed a secret after they learned them. Still thereafter they kept an air of the cabal—even when the churches were opened—by only whispering the Act of Contrition in the confessional, no matter what the priests in later years said they were free to do.

Carmelita was the one who volunteered, publicly and graciously and loudly, to take the two children to the chapel at the hospital. She made it clear that this was an act of bravery as well as generosity, but she didn't need to. For once she was right, and people understood.

She could have taken them to the hospital many ways, but what she chose was absolute. They did not have to walk all dressed in white down the middle of the street the whole way, but they did. They could have taken a taxi, even though they were poor. For this, people took taxis or buses. Not Carmelita.

Not even with the cold and the snow, which came more often in those years to Nogales. There were two trips to be made, one to confession the Saturday afternoon and one to communion early the next Sunday morning.

After their first Saturday expedition, Rosa asked Carmelita,

"But how are you going to take those children? How can you go walking again in the morning, dressed in white like that and with the cold and the snow up to their ankles?"

Carmelita found a way to turn the moment and to be bulldog-like in doing so, saying, "They can't do anything to me, the authorities." She shook her head no.

"But they can, Carmelita, they can do something, they can arrest you."

"No." It was a small word, but big in her mouth. "No, they won't do anything to me," she said, "They can't. I've got my religion, and that's worth something now." With that she put her fist to her chest several times. She took the children again the next morning, in just the same manner, plainly down the streets and to the church, white dress and suit against the white snow, one angel on each side of her.

What the two children would remember more, however, was how they were not allowed to eat after three o'clock on the Saturday afternoon. Only water until after communion, when there would be special cakes and wonders for the mouth, hot chocolate.

Carlos cried to his mother and said, "But I'm so hungry, *Mamá*."

Cuca stuck out her tongue at Carlitos, and he cried even more. Cuca kept mouthing "crybaby" when Carmelita wasn't looking. Carmelita kept swatting him on the top of the head.

The two made their First Communion after all, though it was cold and had in fact snowed through the night, the both of them crying now along the walk down from the hill, through the streets, and a half mile farther, up another hill to the Sacred Heart Church, which is where the priest decided to have communions after all.

The organdy dress and linen suit were wet. The ruffles on Cuca's dress and Carlos's shirtfront did not ruffle, or when they did it was because the two children were shivering.

AFTER AMPARO left the house for the second time, Rosa did not know what to do. She felt weak physically, but in a low voice José said to her, "You are her mother, and you should go looking for her."

"I did go, yesterday," said Rosa.

"Well, you didn't tell me. Rosa, all that's left, we should do it. We'll go and talk to the man and see what he says."

Pancho, the boy himself about whom nobody was saying anything, was in training as a boxer. He had already done well in two very small arranged fights and in a real fight by the field at the far end of the riverbed. That fight had been against a real somebody, a gang boy so mean he had been kicked out of the Plano Oriente in Cajeme and had come here to make his name.

After her Pancho took Amparo away—and she took him, too—after they took each other, and though she was only twenty-five, they killed this Pancho in the ring in Mazatlán, a single blow to the head. The newspapers everywhere reported the death of a "Kid Azteca," and so no one knew, not even his father, until much later.

Amparo was widowed, and after a while, almost by accident, came back to live with her family again, but in the new town, and in a new way. She became the regular chaperon of Cuca, who would also be widowed young, even younger than herself.

JOSÉ AND Rosa did go to speak to the old man, without Amparo and without the boy. They took Cuca along, because who knew what would have to be done, and she would later remember the three of them in front of the theater, knocking, and standing in the wind.

She would remember this in the way she would remember the earlier airplanes: this moment had so much of that peculiar quality of things being bigger than they are. She would remember the old man having come out and standing against a wall, talking to José and Rosa, none of them suggesting going into the empty theater, though they were all shivering.

Cuca had imagined the man to be much bigger than he was when he finally came out. She spent this time taking her hands in and out of her coat, blowing on them for a sort of warmth. She had no real idea what they were talking about and could better hear the trains in the distance.

As they were walking home, Cuca heard Rosa say to José, "Now the hard part comes."

"Then you must make yourself hard," was all he said in response, but with the water from the wind in his eyes he said more, and Cuca and Rosa both heard.

"You are a mother, after all," he said later. "It's like that. Take Cuca with you."

"Yes," said Rosa, and a few days later she and Cuca walked to the municipal courtrooms.

What was noticeable at once was that only the extraordinary came here; this was not a place for the regular. Good or bad, things mattered here. Rosa with her Cuca walked through the doorway, and Rosa crossed herself and whispered a Hail Mary. Cuca, who wanted to know what was the matter, knew better than to ask. One did not interrupt the business of Hail Marys.

Carmelita was already seated in one of the chairs.

Rosa and Cuca sat a distance behind her. When Rosa had made herself comfortable, Carmelita got up—breathing into herself all of the air of the room as she did so—walked back to Rosa, and said, "See now, there will be justice done here, toward that whore of a daughter of yours."

Then she turned, and with her version of equanimity, Carmelita walked back to her chair and sat, put her lips out, and let out a sigh as long as all the air she had taken in before.

Rosa stayed where she was. It felt to her as if there were no place else to go in the room anyway. The magistrate came out, seated himself, and made some comments, too quickly and in words reachable only by ladder, or perhaps standing on one of these chairs, which neither Rosa nor Cuca was willing to do. They simply watched Carmelita, who made a move that was as close to standing on a chair as anyone would want to see.

The magistrate asked something of a general nature, as to

what crime was there here or what matter was to be decided, as he shuffled some papers in front of him.

Carmelita stood and said in a loud voice, without pause, "I want that they should be married first and then put in jail for not being married, and then the boy should be shot. I know the law, I know my rights of request...."

"Calm down, madam, calm down," said the magistrate, waving her back into her seat.

"No sir. You can't tell me to be quiet. I know what's what here...."

All Rosa could do was to be quiet and watch, as if she were her own daughter Cuca, who had gotten up and was standing small against the back wall.

"So you," said the magistrate to Carmelita, "you come forth then as her mother...."

The bailiff said that no, she was not the mother.

"Madam, then can you tell me exactly what is your relation to these young ..."

Before he could finish she said, "I am of course her aunt, so I am sure—"

Before she could go further, he interrupted her loudly. "Madam, sit back in your chair this moment. Where is the mother?"

Rosa was so quiet on the outside that an equal quiet had taken hold on the inside. She did not for a moment understand that she was being called until the bailiff nodded to her, with emphasis.

"What do you ask here of this court for these two people, madam?" asked the magistrate, quite directly at Rosa.

"Well, that they be married."

At that Carmelita jumped up again and in her voice said both to Rosa and to the judge, "No! This is not enough. There should also be punishment, after what has happened here—"

The magistrate himself almost jumped up. "Sit! Now, or you will be removed," he said.

"Well," said Rosa evenly, "if they want to marry, then what's done is done."

"Rosa!" shouted Carmelita. "You can't possibly go along with this, how could this make you happy. . . . "

And with that the bailiff removed Carmelita, trying to put a hand over her mouth. But she did not go willingly, and for a moment because of the high ceilings it seemed as if the bailiff had taken her body but not her mouth. In some manner it was still there, and open.

The boy's grandfather came forth as well, having been standing even more small than Cuca along the back wall. Rosa had not seen him. "If it's what they want."

The magistrate married Amparo and Pancho, and there was some happiness.

BUT THE MOMENT they walked out of the building, Carmelita was waiting for them all.

"You panderer," she said to the old man, looking at him with her nose and with her lips pushed together and out, and then to her sister, "So what? This Amparo and this boy, are their hands made of sugar? The way you and that circus judge in there licked them." She went on and on until it was as if night had confused its place and come in the afternoon.

In the weeks and months afterward, Rosa and her family did not see Amparo in the house anymore.

And they did not know what Carmelita was doing. Amparo and Pancho moved into a very small house at the top of the other side of the hill from Jardín Street, where her parents lived. It might have been nice.

But at the bottom of the street, Carmelita would stand and shout up the small canyon, "Ingrates! We don't want to see you, not me and not your mother, not anybody, not in any of our houses, you devil-people. . . . "

Rosa didn't know this was happening, as not one of her neighbors was rude enough to tell her such a thing. Rosa would come home from work in despair, asking if Amparo had come and wondering why she would not visit. Her prayers became a baby talk when no one was listening, and in them she would talk to Amparo again.

On her days off, Rosa would take Cuca for a walk, but just so that they might simply walk somewhere near Amparo's little house, just so that they might see what there was to be seen. She could not go up to the house and knock herself. It was too much for her, all of this. It couldn't be done. She could not herself be so rude as to intrude on Amparo, but she could not understand why Amparo did not invite her, did not come over. She did not think about Carmelita in all of this. That was the thing about Carmelita. No one had the imagination, or the desire, to see her doing anything more.

Amparo felt herself to be so much of the family that her life here was now an embarrassment for everyone. If Carmelita, with whom she had spent so much time, who had been sometimes her mother, if she was saying these things, then, well.

Amparo and her Pancho disappeared.

When Rosa finally heard, all she could do was cry. She took Cuca and went to look for the old man to ask for an address, but he said he did not have one. And that if he did, he certainly did not wish for this other woman from the day of the courts to have it—she had already come to him to say she would go after them.

No address, he told her, nodding his head. "The boy is my only family," he said, and Rosa could see that he was afraid.

"Carmelita? Was it Carmelita, this woman?" asked Rosa. But he said nothing more.

Rosa was quiet, but not weak. It had never been weakness. Had she known what Carmelita had done, she would have spoken to her immediately. And certainly José would have gone to Carmelita with loud hands if he had known she had come to threaten this man, much less their own daughter.

But for years, because of manners, nobody said anything to Rosa or José about what had happened, what Carmelita had been doing. It just happened. There was no explaining. People understood this.

ROSA AND José did not hear the story of Carmelita's voice in the canyon until they heard it from Amparo herself.

When there had been any money extra, which was never the case but for this she made it happen, Rosa had from time to time put requests for her daughter's whereabouts in the papers. And since Rosa did not speak to Carmelita for the next year and a half because of what happened at the court, she did not know that there was a second half to all this. And Carmelita did not say a thing, even when they did finally speak.

Two years later, some cousins had gone to see Elena and Heráclio in Cajeme, where they had since moved and opened up their new restaurant and hotel. These same cousins happened to be passing through Nogales and stopped to see Rosa as well.

Roberto and Lucas, after a great deal of conversation, said, quietly because they did not know what to expect, "Rosa, did you know we saw Amparo in Cajeme?"

"What do you mean, you saw Amparo?" Rosa had no breath.

"No, well, no, we didn't see her exactly. You know how it is. We just heard that she was there."

"But how," said Rosa, and they gave her the names of some friends—and wasn't this a coincidence, these were friends who had taken part in José and Rosa's own marriage.

"Do you remember?" asked Roberto, but Rosa only wanted to know about Amparo. "Well, these friends, they live in Cajeme now and are doing well as tailors. We think, in fact, that she is living with them," said Lucas, the other cousin.

The story they told was not true, not so easily, as Rosa made a few trips to Cajeme to look for Amparo. It wasn't true, but it was possible. Rosa decided the time had come to take up the offer of Aunt Elena and Uncle Heráclio, who kept saying there was opportunity, *and* telling her how many things she could do, *and* that José would find work in a minute. That they needed her.

José was already disposed to go, as he wanted to follow his former employer from the mortuary, who had given him a great deal of business and who had also moved out there. It was a golden place, the mortician would say, in the way morticians too often do. But José understood, and there were enough people in Cajeme now, certainly, to make the funeral business a good one.

So they moved.

Enough had happened here. Later, the rest of Rosa's sisters would end up moving to Cajeme as well, also to get away.

Carmelita, finally left alone, would—by cards and by letters and by telegrams—follow her adopted son, Carlos, to Los Angeles in her last years to tell him he was ungrateful and she would refuse to die no matter what the doctors told her.

ROSA COULD not find Amparo after the move, but she looked. She continued to put announcements in the newspapers of the area, in Cócori, in Esperanza, in Navojoa, in Alamos. She never thought Amparo had gone very far, that she had to be somewhere. It was like when Amparo was in the little house after she married. Rosa did not see her, but she knew Amparo was there. It was something. It was a little bit of something to feel. Perhaps as far as Hermosillo, Rosa would think, or around there.

When Cuca was fifteen, Rosa received a letter. Rosa had taken on a fever, which seemed to be on the rise over a week, but the letter came to her like water. There was no coincidence, said Rosa later.

"It's me, your daughter," the letter said. After so many years, eight, and this was the first letter. Amparo had sent it to general delivery, and by the habit of all the years Rosa would check the list of unaddressed letters every week, until finally this came. A list of names would always be posted, and it called to her.

"It's me, your daughter, Amparo," the letter said. That it had been a few months now since her Pancho had been killed boxing, how when he died he was someone else, Kid Azteca, and in that moment so was she someone else. She wanted to come home to her mother, and she asked about the other children, and her father, who might not want her.

But when Amparo arrived, they were all waiting, all dressed up, José with his suit.

Everything was different. This was all without Carmelita. And it was that kind of meeting: Amparo herself was all dressed up, and the children wanted to touch her because she seemed so beautiful, but they could not, because they did not know her, so tall and thin.

Cuca in those days did not know what to expect. She was the only one of the children to have been part of what happened, and so the only one who knew something. But Amparo hugged her, and kissed her, and then Cuca was glad that she knew. Her sister was her sister, finally and again, and they could not have enough of each other, nor Amparo of all of them.

"But I don't want to live in the house," said Amparo. It was not cruelty in her voice. It was calm. "I want to work. I have only very little experience, but I want to find something. Please."

Rosa was already an experienced helper in the kitchens of this town and said that she could perhaps find Amparo some work in that regard. "But you will live here, at home. This is where you belong."

They made a compromise, Amparo sometimes staying in a small room she had found in one of the shops downtown and some-times at home. It was better this way, a little bit of everything.

The work she did, in fact, for the next year was with Cuca in the family's backyard, taking care of the fifty chickens and the eight pigs, which were their numbers more or less. In this work Amparo found her genius for those months. She and Cuca were the only ones in charge, as José, though he was home more than Rosa in those days, could not bring himself to do this kind of work.

Amparo killed the chickens when there was a need and made the *chicharrones* from leftover beef, and when the pigs came of age, she learned what to do. She began to do this work for Elena and Heráclio's restaurant as well, learning to take the leftovers from the plates of the customers and to mix this into a feed for the animals, a mix of corn and salt so that the animals were always fat.

Because of the story from the family's cousins about staying with the tailors who were part of her parents' wedding and vaguely related because of someone named Graciela, Amparo did in fact become friends with them. And after a time, they offered her the job she was supposed to have had at the beginning of the story.

When Amparo saw what the work was, the cutting of materials and the forms they took, it did not seem unlike the taking into parts of one of the pigs or chickens, and so she said yes.

"Mind you, as a helper," they said, "just a helper."

Rosa was agreeable to the arrangement as well, saying that it suited her. "But she doesn't know how to sew," said Rosa to the tailors, just so that everything was out in the open. Amparo put her head down, but Rosa said to her quietly, "This sewing, it might be a touchy thing with tailors."

But they said it was all right, since they could not pay her very much. It was a place to learn, they all agreed, and Amparo was happy with the possibility of a new life, if only a small new life. She did not need more than that.

At first, her job was to be the cleaner, because a tailor shop in those days did both. The cleaning section of the shop was in back, a crude setting, a wooden table, a bucket of water, and a bucket of gasoline.

Amparo's job was to first get the soiled garment and brush it, very well, very hard. Then the brush was dipped in the water and then in the gasoline, and the garment was again brushed, very well, very hard, a good rasping. The garment was next hung in the sun, three or four hours, to try and get rid of some of the gasoline smell, then, if it survived, it was taken inside and ironed.

A customer had to hope for the best and that the remaining

smell would not be too much. "With a little wear," the tailors would say over and over, "the smell goes away. Don't worry."

In later years came the Clorox and the soap from stores, things that didn't smell so much or else smelled better.

But Amparo had good eyes, and there were four tailors at work in this place, so she could not help but take note of what they were doing and how they did it. Soon they were letting her do one thing and then another, and to a one they were admiring of her sure hand. It had the mark of a firm muscle.

"Chickens and pigs," she would say, and laugh. But the tailors didn't understand. They would just shake their heads.

Within three years, however, she had a small graduation one Friday, with a small cake and hors d'oeuvres that everyone picked up with pins. Amparo had now become a tailor of both men's and women's suits, with a particular specialty in the wedding dress.

"Because of love," she would say, and mean it many ways.

PERHAPS the wedding dresses were what drew Amparo and Cuca together. When no one else was in the shop, Amparo would let Cuca try on the particular dress she was making. They would tell each other a made-up story of the two people who would be marrying, and what the wedding and their lives together would be like. The stories always ended with either Moorish castles and a princess or else a gruesome murder with blood all over the dress, blood that even gasoline could not remove, blood forming into meaningful designs, into the name of the killer, but always as an anagram. The woman's blood was always a good friend to her, but a bad speller.

"Blood," said Amparo, "it gives you trouble even after you die." And with this, the both of them would laugh and pass through the hours of the day easily. None of their stories was concerned with anything in between. Made-up stories are like that, all good or all bad.

That's when Cuca told Amparo about Celso, who was neither.

It was to be a first date, and Cuca could not help but be embarrassed talking about such a thing. But Amparo understood, and agreed immediately to be the one who would accompany her to the movie theater—Amparo knew about theaters, after all— and would not let Cuca think twice about saying no.

"Listen, *mañeca*," the boy had said to Cuca, but he was really a man, "listen, I'll wait for you outside the theater, and I'll buy the tickets already, and we'll go in together. You bring your sister. All right?"

"Yes," said Cuca, that simple. It was the shortest thing she could think to say. "Yes." She almost could not even say that. The embarrassment, that's all she could think. It filled her.

Cuca by now was sixteen and worked in the Cities of France, a store that had a little of everything, but only a little. The store was very small. She would normally leave work in the late afternoon, and what had happened was that Celso had waited for her outside the shop and already knew everything about her. He was a man already and very much older than Cuca, so she had to listen to him.

"Your sister Amparo, you tell her to come along, all right," he said. He gave her no room to say otherwise. It was not a question. There was no question mark at the end of it. Not this time.

"Don't worry, I know you. I know who your parents are. You know, *mañeca*, if you paid attention to me, I would marry you." With that he winked at her, and cocked his head.

Cuca didn't know what to do. She had seen him around before, but that was all, and had not thought much of it. Not that she was surprised, entirely. The woman who ran the store next to the Cities of France had told her that there was a man who lived next to her house who had told her he would do just that. He would marry Cuca, he said, if she would just pay attention to him. But Cuca had only laughed then.

She did not make herself up like the other girls yet or dress like them. She wore striped socks and brown shoes. She didn't go to dances or any of that. So all she could do when this woman told her was to laugh it off. And that was all Amparo could do as well when Cuca told her.

Amparo by this time went to all the dances and knew everyone else who went. She couldn't believe what Cuca was telling her. Cuca? She still saw her little sister as exactly that, and when Amparo had given her money to go to the movies, it was to go to the movies. Very simple, nothing more, and always only the matinee, two o'clock in the afternoon. Amparo for a moment saw herself as her own mother, or worse. That was why she agreed right away to take Cuca.

"But who is he?" Cuca had asked of the woman, and Amparo wanted to know the same thing.

There had been another boy interested in Cuca before this, Ysidro, who had worked in the restaurant of Aunt Elena, who one afternoon had told her, "*Güerita* Cuca, do you want to come out with me?"

Cuca even then had said nothing, had not even answered him. This was the first boy, and he had said the same things as this new one.

"Look," he said, "my name is Ysidro. You like me, I think, very much. So why not?"

Cuca always looked older than her true age. When she was fifteen, she looked eighteen at least, except for her face. It was a confusion both for her and for others. This was especially so in that she did not yet have conversation. She had the rest, but not words.

"Meet me at the *cortina* of trees," said Ysidro, and she could not say anything, not even no.

"I'll be there waiting," he said. Then he added, because this was a town of manners, "And bring somebody who will come with you." It was manners, or else he knew this was the only way he could get her to meet him. It was manners that much.

Cuca told Amparo then too.

"*Ayyy*, sister," said Amparo, and she teased Cuca with a shaking of the head and a clucking of the tongue against the teeth.

"My little sister. My, my, my." Amparo went on and on. But she took Cuca to the *cortina* of trees anyway. It was a game then, this first time. It was like the stories of the wedding dresses. They went to see if this story would end high in a castle or down in a pool of blood. It was a good game between sisters.

They sat on one of the several benches and they waited. Amparo could not sit still. "So when is this boy going to come, anyway? I don't think he's going to come; I don't know." She tapped her foot melodramatically.

All Cuca could do was be embarrassed and put her head down.

"Oh, don't look like a cow with your head down like that," said Amparo, "or he'll never come!"

Cuca put her head down even more. She meant to put her head up, but it didn't work right. If the boy Ysidro came now, he would have to know Cuca by her hair or her legs because she could show nothing of her face. Her whole body was not working right.

The boy did arrive, and was attractive on this Sunday, said Amparo later. She liked him, and in fact the boy was more her age.

Ysidro sat next to them. "Good afternoon," he said politely.

Amparo, who was sitting on the opposite side, kept nudging Cuca. "Introduce me, introduce me," she whispered, but Cuca could not speak, not at all. Her head was still refusing to work. She wanted to talk, but nothing would move.

"It's just that for her," said Amparo, talking directly to the boy Ysidro and motioning with her eyes at Cuca, "for her it's the first time."

Cuca moaned, or mooed as Amparo later said to her. Some sound from the farm animals. "I knew keeping your head down like that would lead to no good." Amparo mimicked the sound.

Ysidro said he understood, and stayed the afternoon with

them, a couple of hours. But the conversation was slight, more between Ysidro and Amparo, and Cuca never saw him again.

THEY HEARD an occasional mention of the boy, once about him going to the Plano Oriente and getting lost, so they laughed.

People only ever whispered when they talked about that section of town, but this story of Ysidro trying to become a man over there—that's what was said—was too much. Cuca wasn't quite sure what this meant—becoming a man—but she could not say so, even to Amparo. So she laughed the hardest.

Any mention thereafter of the boy made them both laugh, but it meant something more. His name in some manner came to mean for them something about which they could not talk but that felt good to say, enough to make them happy and to laugh. *Ysidro*. It came to mean "becoming a man," but it had nothing to do with men.

Amparo had heard the story from some friends of hers who lived there. She didn't care who knew it. Still, she herself talked about the place only in whispers, even to Cuca. But after a while and through the years, the whispers just sounded like regular talk.

In the Plano Oriente, Amparo would tell Cuca, people still made houses of reed grass and of mud, with earthen roofs, and all the commotion on the other side of town did not mean so much here. This place was also more mysteriously, and in whispers, sometimes called El Congal, and was taboo for people on the other side.

When someone would say that someone else had gone to the Plano Oriente the night before—well, at first, no one was quite sure what that meant. From the distance one could make out a gathering of perhaps fifty structures out there. After a few years, one heard in conversations certain advice: *If you want to enjoy yourself, go over there.*

Later one began to understand that the men went there to the appointment houses, the *congales*, which is where the prostitutes were, who could not then come over to the Cajeme side. It was rumored they needed special permissions from the Health Department and that they were checked once a week, an examination of who knew what dimension. Only after this—or the quiet exchange of money—were the permissions given out, in the form of identification cards.

At first, these women had no place in Cajeme, and so the townspeople tried to ignore them in the best way they could: with paper and with forms, with regulations, hoping they would go away or that the men would simply not visit them.

The women there lived the lives, some said, of lepers, but opposite: everyone touched them. Nonetheless, like lepers, they were not free to move about. In the early days of this town, as well, there was so much courtesy, so many manners, so much concern for propriety, that these things happened. In wanting to start out on the right foot, the town built itself out of a book, with page numbers and chapters and all the rules. But it was a cookbook, and some cakes do not rise in the manner described therein. That's when the Plano Oriente started. It was a cake that leaned a little to the left, no matter what.

It didn't last that way, of course, but in those days there were absolutes. No fairy tales. In the beginning, the only ones who went over to the Plano Oriente with propriety were the various vendors who sold clothing and assorted goods.

After a while, however, small businesses with permanent structures began to spring up, as a great deal of money came into this section of town and business here was good. With money, people began to cross over, and the wide lines between Cajeme and this place began to be covered over with mud like the regular streets.

Mud itself became self-important, a braggart and a bully, a thief, as in time the curtain of trees was found not to protect the proper part of Cajeme. When the rains came, the town of Cajeme proper flooded almost into a lake. As more people went over to the Plano Oriente, sometimes just to get dry, the great plan of the town, described and designed by the architects and philosophers of the day, fell apart. Nobody lived where they were supposed to, and nobody had taken that into account.

The curtain of trees itself should have told them something. How could they have named it this, the *cortina*, and therefore think themselves comfortable? Certainly it was something half civilized in the curtain, but still as well half wild in the trees. Drawing closed a curtain does not, as the children wanted to believe at the circus and in the living rooms of favorite uncles, make a thing disappear. For a minute, maybe. Even an hour.

But the town had only played a big joke on itself with this curtain and after a while began to learn how to live with all of its parts, right and left, up and down. But the change was very slow. Even after years, for example, if a young woman were found pregnant before marriage, she no longer existed. That was the real curtain. And there were other, more subtle certainties. They were meant to be manners, courtesies, and even kindnesses. But often they were not.

Rules, written or not, were very simple that way at first and easy, so not everyone wanted to go along with the changes. Who knew, after all, what the changes would mean?

"No manners," people would say about this or that, and shake their heads. "Just a year ago, who would have thought?"

"BUT WHAT was this man's name?" Cuca asked of the lady who had told her about the neighbor, the man who was interested now.

"Celso Rojo is his name. He's older, but he's still, well, you know, a boy," she said. The woman looked at Cuca in a way to make the words mean more, but Cuca didn't understand.

"Is he married or something? I mean, that is, has he been married? He looks older to me," said Cuca.

"He's had very many women, girlfriends, but he's never been married. He lives with his mother." Cuca wasn't sure but thought that these words were supposed to mean more as well.

Four or five days after their talk, a man walked by the front of the Cities of France, wearing overalls that said "Ford," full of grease.

"*Mañeca,*" he said to Cuca, casually but not so as to be mistaken as being addressed to someone else, "*adiós.*" He said the word in that way of making the word mean "hello"—not "good-bye" at all. And he said it with a Castilian accent from his father, which made the word not only mean its opposite but gave an air of mystery as well. He was not saying good-bye with his *adiós* at all. Even Cuca understood this time.

But *mañeca*—what did that mean? Did it mean *muñeca,* doll? No, that was too much. She was not a girl like that. That was a word from the other side of town. It had to be something else. It was something from the accent, something else. But she could not be so rude as to ask him to explain.

Tall and well shaped, attractive, one of those men who was just one of those men. Cuca wasn't sure what that meant when she said it to herself, but she could sense that what he was in that moment wasn't something for the head. He spoke to some other part of her.

But he looked so much older, thought Cuca, and so polished, even in those overalls.

"Dirty old man!" said Cuca, and she waved him off as if he were a fly.

But later in the day, as Cuca was getting ready to close the shop just after lunch, the woman from the store next door shouted "*Güera, güera,* come here!" The woman called Cuca over to the door of her adjoining shop, where she worked.

"Do you see that man, the one over there?"

Cuca looked and saw a man standing with some others who were all dressed in the fashionable white linen suits of the day. They wore white linen no matter what, no matter how much mud there might be in the streets, no matter how much heat or cold. They wore the white linen suits together with their *saracof* hats, which were white and low, more like pith helmets than hats. These hats were popular in those days, but their popularity lasted only a few years into the forties. Nobody would remember them after that, not even the dictionaries. It was a fever of peculiar men's hats in those days, and the women wanted them gone. If only, they would say, if only the men would try something Panamanian, something like that. But that's the way men were.

Celso by association had a share in the elegance of the town square and the young men who were gathered, although he was still dressed in his overalls. How did he do this? wondered Cuca.

As she walked by, *"Adiós, mañeca,"* he said again, in his manner. But this time they were flowers, these words. Something in them made Cuca rise a little, as if she had caught on to some little hook in those words, something hidden in the flowers that would not let her go. Her head rising instead of falling? This felt like some kind of trick.

"LISTEN," SAID Amparo to Cuca, "there's going to be a piñata for Mario, so why don't you stop over and eat a little?" And she added, because she still saw Cuca in this way, "There will be candy, after all. For everybody."

Mario was the little son of Ramona and Don Jesús Partida, and they were making a cake and all the rest of a fuss for his eleventh birthday.

"At least go before it finishes and get some candy for you and Chelo," said Amparo. Chelo was the next youngest sister in the Martínez family after Cuca.

And the mention of the candies did, in fact, convince her. That afternoon after work, Cuca went to the party and saw Amparo, ate some cake, and saw that the piñata had already been broken. But Amparo had saved her three napkinsful of candies, one for Cuca, one for Chelo, and one even for Guille, who was next after Chelo in line.

"Now make sure you eat only this one that's for you," said Amparo. Cuca made a face as if to say to Amparo, You didn't have to say that.

But Amparo did. As Cuca walked down the street toward her

house, she ate her part of the candies as quickly as she could so that she would be able to finish off the others before she got home. She packed her mouth and could not quite keep it closed, giving her an involuntary half smile.

Cuca had not seen Celso at the party, but he was there.

And he came walking after her. *"Buenas tardes, mañeca,"* he said in that way of his.

Cuca could say nothing. That was both how she felt and all she could do anyway, as her mouth was otherwise fully at work. She would not have known what to say in any regard. He had his own linen suit on now, not the overalls, but it made no real difference. He had looked good even before. Cuca didn't know what to do.

No one had ever spoken to her before. Not like this, not this kind of *buenas tardes.* There had been boys, they knew how to say it this way, but that was from the playgrounds. Here was a man, from maybe the upper class. A dirty pair of overalls meant, after all, that there was, first, a car to be worked upon. And someone had to own it.

Cuca didn't know what to do. She had been given no training. Her mother had said nothing. Amparo just teased her. The churches were just barely opening, and no one yet spoke openly there. Her friends all worked, as she did, and one after another fell into something with someone, but always a boy.

This was a man. No amount of giggling or whispering was a help here.

"Buenas tardes, mañeca," he said again, and Cuca lowered her head. Even though it was Celso, lowering her head was easier this time, because it was all mouth and weighed something from all of the candies she had put in. Cuca could say nothing.

"You know," he said, "I saw you leave the party. And I followed you."

Cuca just kept walking.

"My name is Celso Rojo. And I think you like me very much."

Cuca felt not only the largeness of her mouth but the redness of its extremities now as well. She didn't know if the redness was from having so much in her mouth or from what he said.

"I know your name. You are Refugio Martínez, and they call you Cuca. You live with your two little sisters and your older sister, Amparo. On Jardín Street."

Cuca, who was embarrassed to begin with about the candy in her mouth, now could not chew, because there it would be, the chewing.

Celso kept talking and walking along with her. "I know you," he said, and nodded some kind of understanding nod. Where does somebody learn something like that? wondered Cuca. How could he nod, and how could that nod show that he knew? It did, in fact—but how could it?

"Sooner or later you will learn about all my secrets, but I will tell them to you now, so that there are no surprises."

Cuca was still quiet. "But I'm talking so much," Celso said. "Why aren't you saying anything? Did the rats eat your tongue? Come on, lift your head up." With that he reached for her chin.

"What do you have in your mouth? Let's see." Cuca said nothing but raised her head a little. Not because she wanted to.

"Well, it's the piñata. I see," said Celso, with a seriousness she didn't know how to take. "You've got the whole piñata right there in your mouth. And these candies were supposed to be for your little sisters, I bet."

Cuca thought he knew everything. All she could do was nod her head, yes, quickly.

"Well, never mind. So, do you want to go to the movies with me?" He gave Cuca no time to answer, no time to chew. He was very clever, thought Cuca.

"You tell your sister to come with you, and I'll wait for you both. On Thursday. All right?" He sounded like the first boy, Ysidro, in that there was no question in his request. The question mark in his voice was just a formality. Maybe he was a little nicer.

Cuca lowered her head farther than before. "On Thursday," he said again, "I'll be waiting for you with the tickets."

Cuca raised her head a little, and then a lot. She could see in the distance her father coming along the street, and in spite of herself she said so—*my father*—as best she could, a little watery.

Celso could see him too. "I know, I know, *mañeca*, how it is. On Thursday," he said, "I'll see you." And he left in the other direction.

Cuca didn't sleep. A man that handsome, she thought. And so big and so well dressed. She didn't sleep, but she dreamed. And it was like all her dreams. This was the stuff of her dreams. The accurate circumstance and details mattered little.

After so many dreams and for so long, how could she not believe that such a thing as this was possible?

CUCA A DAY later told Amparo that she had been asked to the movies, and wouldn't she go with her, please?

"Little sister, little sister, *ayyy*," she said, and teased Cuca again. "Just like with that boy Ysidro," Amparo noted, more with a nod of the head than with the words she said. They had not talked much about Ysidro since he disappeared.

"But who is this one?" asked Amparo. "Who is he? Do I know him?"

"Well," said Cuca, "he just said to tell you that he would see us on Thursday at the movies, that he would wait for us there with tickets."

"I'll take you, of course I'll take you," said Amparo. "I'll go to the house on Thursday, but don't you say a word to those parents of yours. I'll go and I'll just say I'm taking you out, and we won't say anything more."

They both knew better than to even think about telling their parents. Rosa and José had had enough with movies and boys to last a very long time.

Amparo came for Cuca as planned, and they went off to the Cine Cajeme. On arriving, Cuca thought he had chosen a Thursday carefully, as it was clearly a family night. The line was very long, but in the distance, on the other side of the crowd, Celso stood holding some tickets.

"Where is he," asked Amparo, "which one?" Cuca couldn't tell if she felt excitement or nervousness. Amparo was just excited.

"It's that one," said Cuca. She pointed with her head and her eyes toward Celso. "That one over there."

"Which one? Wait, Cuca, aren't you mistaken?"

"No, he's the one."

"Cuca, that's not him, I don't think. Maybe he's with those boys over there?"

"No, that's him. It's the one you're looking at. He said he was going to wait for us and have the tickets already in his hands, and there he is. What should we do?"

Amparo asked again, "Are you sure that's the one? Him?" The sound of Amparo's talking didn't sound as purely excited as it had earlier.

"Yes, yes." Cuca squeezed her eyes to say yes with them, too.

"I don't know. That one's a little old for you, maybe. Well, if he doesn't come over here, we'd better go over to him. If you're sure he's the one. Go on, Cuca. Go on." Amparo seemed a little breathless, a little unsure, even if her words said otherwise. It was a contagious feeling, and Cuca caught it, even stronger than what she already felt.

"But I don't want to." Cuca had already put her head down, which was how it felt best these last few days before tonight.

"What is this?" asked Amparo. "Is this what you brought me here for, to waste my time? What do you mean, you don't want to?"

"Well, I'm just embarrassed. That's all."

"Don't be ridiculous, Cuca. Go on, walk over to him. I'll come with you; now go on. Nobody's going to bite you."

The words sounded strong, but they only scared Cuca more.

"But I don't want to." Cuca could not put her head any lower.

"You're going to give me the gray hairs. Embarrassed. What kind of a thing is that to say now? I don't believe this." And with that, Amparo stood in line and bought new tickets, all as Celso stood where he was, with his own set of tickets in his hands.

Celso would say later that he didn't want to come closer because he was afraid Amparo was going to say something. She had the look in her eye. He came closer as they entered because he could hear Amparo getting mad at Cuca. Close, but not too close. He understood about these things.

"There," said Amparo as they were entering, "are you happy now that you've made me buy tickets, made me waste my money on this? And this invention of yours, this boy, I don't think there is any boy at all, I think you're mistaken." Amparo went on and on this way, and Cuca just put her head down as they walked all the way to the seats.

"Why didn't you just say you wanted to come to the movies? I would have brought you anyway. I can't believe you. . . . "

"But it was him," said Cuca.

"Then why didn't he come up to us? Why didn't he come and tell me that?"

In that instant they both heard from behind, *"Buenas noches,"* as Celso put his head between the two of them.

"Buenas noches," he said again, and they acknowledged him with a small nod, not speaking anymore. That was the way these things worked.

"Miss," Celso said to Amparo, "do you know that I have an interest in your sister?"

"Well, yes, she told me. I just didn't know."

"I bought the tickets but didn't want to seem rude. I didn't want to just intrude on you by walking right over. I didn't know what you would think."

"It's just that it's her first time," said Amparo, looking at Cuca, who was still embarrassed but who gave a little smile back to Amparo anyway, for Ysidro. A smile, but also a small moan, in remembrance.

It occurred to Cuca in that moment what had happened with Ysidro. She had not been able to say anything to him, not anything much, and he had talked about the beauty of the sky, the timbre of the birdsongs, and the distance of the horizon. Then, from nerves maybe, he had picked up a sprig of some sort from the grasses that grew around the *cortina* of trees, grasses that had overreached a little from the great gardens of Lamberto Díaz. He put the sprig in his mouth. He moved it around with his lips and his teeth, and laughed a little.

But at that Cuca blurted out that he looked like a burro eating from the trough full of slop. Just like that. A finger snap.

Amparo at that moment tried her best and said to Ysidro, "You know, it's just that she's never gone out with anyone." Amparo shrugged her shoulders for Cuca.

"I know," said the boy.

"I KNOW," said Celso.

"Never with a boy before at all," Amparo said.

"I know. But I wonder, would you do me the favor," said Celso formally, "of letting me sit with the two of you?"

"Of course," said Amparo. With that he came and sat next to Cuca, putting her in the middle of the three. He and Amparo continued to talk, and Cuca kept her head down as she sat between them.

The movie began, *Chucho, el Roto,* and they all watched until it finished. It was about a real man who was a Robin Hood character. "*Chucho*" was his name, and "*roto*," something broken or shattered, was both his disguise and his badge. Celso turned to Cuca. "Did you like it?"

"Yes," said Cuca. That was all. It was the most she had said, and even then she spoke quietly.

"All right, then. Let's go out and get something to eat," he said, almost as part of a laugh. It was a half laugh and half statement, so that before Cuca and Amparo knew it, they were laughing too, which meant *all right.*

They were close to home, and getting back would not take

long. And anyway, Cuca was with Amparo. That's what everyone thought. Just Amparo, so that nobody would be worried.

Cuca never went out much at this time of night with anyone, and all she could think of was how much it was like the very early morning, before there was any light at all. That's when she and her mother would walk to the *mercado*, and her mother would talk about the sisters in the stars and they would look at the face in the moon together. It was their way of looking at each other.

And there was a crisp smell, a watery smell, not wet, but just right. Just something. Just enough to let them know they were two human beings awake and in council with the inner workings of nature. There was no noise, but it was all noise, all life, everything about to get up. In this way, they walked inside a dream, along a pathway, which, at that time of the morning, was the twenty minutes before rising, before people open their eyes.

Celso, Amparo, and Cuca went to eat at a little restaurant, which again embarrassed Cuca. It was a sit-down restaurant, and Cuca wanted to say, almost as a joke this time, but it was not a joke, *Celso, this is my first time.* She had eaten with her father at the stands and places like that. But this was one of the restaurants around the *mercado*, and they were for other people.

Cuca ordered one tostada only, and even then, the thought of how much it might cost, just for a tostada, it was almost too much to bear. What would he think of her? she wondered. Cuca tried to eat it when he was not looking and tried to enjoy it, but she felt full already from so much worry.

Then they were done at last, and Celso walked them the several blocks toward their house.

"Don't walk up to the fence, please," Amparo said to Celso. "You know. He might be waiting up for us, standing in the yard." She did not need to use names.

"Don't worry," said Celso. "But I am coming to visit. You may count on it. I will come to ask permission, of course, to see, you know—," and with that he nodded his head at Cuca.

"Now?" blurted Amparo, who could not believe it. "Don't be a fool! Not now. It's so late. Who's ever heard of such a thing—"

"I want to visit *mañeca*'s house. I want to marry her. It's that simple. I'm just losing time."

Through all this, no one spoke to Cuca, nor did she speak up.

"Don't be crazy," said Amparo. "It's been one day, one evening."

"No," said Celso, "it's something serious with me about her."

"We don't even know who you are." Amparo did not know whether to laugh or to take him seriously. This time it was Amparo's turn to feel the mix of excitement and nervousness. Cuca only felt numb.

With her head down, Cuca had begun to smile. It was all she could do. It was like having all that candy in her mouth. What did she need to know? she thought. This was just how the dreams said it would go.

The three of them walked toward the house.

AMPARO WAS a girl for the parties. As a result, it was this same October of Cuca and Celso that Amparo met Rafael, on San Rafael's day. Cuca and Celso had gone out together for a few weeks now, in hiding. Amparo had convinced Celso to wait after all, to have some patience.

This was just another of the town's small parties, a regular one, an easy place to go unnoticed. It was the kind of gathering where, in the past, Amparo walked away friends with everyone, the opposite of Cuca.

The occasion was one in a line of parties for saints' days, baptisms, weddings, always outside in somebody's watered-down yard. There was so much food, and always *tesguino*, because it was the cheapest and the best thing to drink, made of pineapple and *panocha* sugar. One could get drunk, working a little at it. But there were sodas as well, and a Victrola, and dancers. Sometimes there was beer or the tequilas out by the wall with the men who got tired of the party if it was for children.

To this one particular party, given for the birthday of a friend of Amparo's, they were all invited. As always, Celso was the center of everything, people all around him. It was his place in life. One after another joke or bit of news, he kept the partygoers all on his lip, all of them with their mouths open. A dancer, and a singer, and a talker—there was nothing at a party he could not do.

Celso was even a musician of sorts and could play the piano and virtually all the stringed instruments. Wherever he went, he would sit in for a time with the musicians and was a great favorite. He had thought early on he would be a musician exclusively but had to drop those plans when he began his work with the Ford car company, who valued him because he moved in and out of all the levels and jobs of the company in much the same way as he was capable with the instruments. Still, he was a lifelong member of the musicians' union. And who knew, he would say, maybe sometime.

Dora, the beneficiary of this party, as it ended said to Amparo that the next day there was to be another party, a saint's day, for a boy, very special. His mother, Doña Manuela, was putting it on, and his name was Rafael Russo. He was out on one of the ranches right now, but when he got home tomorrow, his mother wanted to give him a surprise party.

"Well, let's all go to it," said Amparo to Celso.

"Certainly, don't you think so, *mañeca?*"

"Yes," said Cuca, and so it was decided. Two parties were not so many.

The mother of the boy Rafael had a cloud in her eye and she was short, and it was only a surprise party of sorts, with everyone putting up their arms as Rafael showed up, though he had seen them all from a distance, and they had seen him.

"Very handsome, very cowboy, like a doll," said Amparo, but quietly, to Cuca. Amparo almost never spoke quietly.

Rafael hugged his mother and thanked her for the party, then went around to each guest and shook hands and introduced himself, bringing sodas as well. The music started, and then the dancing could not help itself. Celso danced with Amparo because Cuca did not know how.

Celso would, several weeks later, bring Cuca her first pair of high heels, maroon, with a matching maroon coat, and he would say, "I want you to wear these."

"But Celso," Cuca would respond, "I can't wear these, not these."

"You must. When I marry you I want to marry a woman, not a little girl."

Cuca would many years later remember that remark and be grateful to him for making her wear the shoes. Grateful, however, she would also say, is only something a little girl who knows nothing better would say.

It was New Year's Eve, and he said, "Put them on now. Tonight."

Amparo said, "It's true, you've got to learn. It's all right."

With this Cuca put on the shoes. But she wanted her socks, and these didn't fit right at all. The world looked a little different from a height.

Celso made her walk in them, and with her ankles they folded over on her, and she began to cry while everyone else laughed. Cuca became so mortified that she felt tears not simply falling but jumping out from her eyes, and she ran to the next room, running out of the shoes as she went. Amparo went to comfort her.

"*Mañeca*, come back, *mañeca*," said Celso.

But it sounded insulting to Cuca, offensive. "Come back to what?"

Amparo pulled her into the room again, and Celso held her in his arms, and he said, "Look, *mañeca*, this is not to hurt you. You'll be glad someday. Not now, I know. You don't understand. But one day you'll be glad."

It took many years.

AFTER THE musicians began to play at Rafael's party and the dancing followed, Amparo said again to Cuca, "That's a handsome boy. I wish he would ask me to dance. If only he would."

Cuca and Amparo were sitting together, as Celso had gone to play the saxophone with the band.

Rafael did come toward them. Just quick, like that.

"Shall we dance?" But he asked Cuca, not Amparo.

"I don't know how," said Cuca. "But dance with my sister." She looked at Amparo, who smiled.

Rafael did dance with Amparo, and he did not leave her, dancing all the rest of the dances only with her. When the party was ended, Rafael asked Celso if he might accompany the three of them on their walk home.

It was the custom to ask in that way, and Rafael wanted to do this correctly. He had no way of knowing that Celso was not officially going out with Cuca, not yet. Celso had not yet himself asked for permission. Usually there was a mother to ask, but Amparo filled that role this night. Nonetheless Celso gave permission to Rafael to come along, and no one said a thing. All that mattered was that permission had been asked for and granted.

Celso joked as they walked and moved this way and that, rolling his head around to make everyone laugh and to put them at ease. Celso was feeling good, and when they were close to the house, he said to Cuca, "When am I going to visit?

"Look, *mañeca*, I want to go to your house and ask permission to see you so that we might marry. But first I want your parents to see me so that they'll know what I'm like. And they should know how I've been, but also how I will be."

"Later," said Cuca, "another time."

"But when?"

Amparo and Cuca did not tell Celso that their parents already knew.

José had charged Rosa with speaking to Amparo, and one day Rosa said to her, "What have you done, why have you let this happen? I've left you in charge of Cuca and look what you've let happen. I know what's happening, I know she's seeing a married man. . . . "

"He's not married, *Mamá*," said Amparo.

"Well, he has been with women, everybody knows. Nineteen, they say, they all say that, from everywhere, all the way from Nogales to who knows where. He's bound to have family, a wife, two wives, a man like that. . . . "

José cut in from the table where he was sitting, pretending not to hear. But he could not help himself.

"The day this man comes around, I'm going to run him off! I don't want him around here. And that is what I say!" José was angry and could not contain himself. It had not been enough to let Rosa do the talking this time.

This had gone on for two weeks at least, the shouting and the talking, and then more shouting. And though no one spoke directly to Cuca, she was the one most afraid.

"Don't come yet, Celso. My father will send you away. I'm sure he will."

"But it's all I can do. I want them to know me."

José had said to Rosa that this man would want to come into their house just to make fun of them, just to ridicule them, in the way he had done with the parents of all these other girls. And he would not have it. He would run him off! In this moment, Cuca could hear her father saying these things as if he were there shouting in her ear.

Celso turned his attention to Amparo and Rafael, and joked with Cuca, "Ahh, so we've finally found someone for skinny Amparo," and he made them all laugh. And a few more weeks went by. Just like that.

BUT THE TIME came when something had to be done. Celso no longer simply waited for Cuca and Amparo at the movie theater. He waited now just a little distance from the fence of their house. He would make jokes and stake out his territory, saying he knew that the inside of the fence was out of bounds but that anything outside it was his.

One Saturday night, however, he said, "All right now. I'm tired of this. I can't wait anymore. Tomorrow I'm coming to talk to your father."

Cuca began to cry because she was afraid. She could imagine so many versions of what might happen, all bad. Without exception.

"You can't go," she said to Celso. "They'll kick you out." She meant her words.

"I'm going," said Celso, who meant his words as well. "Now don't worry. Don't make yourself sick." This made Cuca feel like a little girl again, and she didn't like it. But she liked that he was going. It was a confusion of things, but for the first time she did not feel like putting her head down.

When Cuca and Celso joined Amparo and Rafael, Celso said what he was going to do.

"Well, then," said Rafael, "I want to go too." He nodded a *yes, it's true* to Amparo. And he and Celso shook hands, half joking, but with a look as well between them.

Cuca didn't know what she would do with herself that night. She could leave the house, out the back, like Amparo had done years earlier. It had worked for Amparo, more or less.

Sunday afternoon at three o'clock precisely, a knock came at the Martínez door.

Rosa had not gathered herself yet and was still uncombed from the housework, in her housedress. On Sundays she always bathed later in the day, to get ready for the evening. Cuca was outside, in back, but she heard. They all heard. It was a knock, clear and to the point. It could not be mistaken.

"Buenas tardes, señora."

Cuca looked around the side of the house and then ran, just ran to the back. Three o'clock in the afternoon, she thought. It wasn't even four. It wasn't even anything. It was three o'clock. God.

Rosa went to look for her in back and said, "Cuca. Cuca, come with me," in a low voice. "You are being called for."

It was Celso, and when Cuca saw him she was embarrassed, but so much more than any of the other times, which themselves had seemed insupportable. There was nothing to do, and Celso shrugged his shoulders to say, *This is the way it is.*

"This man has come to ask permission to see you," said Rosa, "but I've told him your father is not here right now. He will be back this evening." She said this to Cuca but meant it for Celso.

"*Mañeca,*" Celso said to Cuca, "I've come to ask. I will come back tonight and speak to your father. What time?" he asked Rosa.

"He will be here by six," she said, polite but without expression.

"I'll come at eight, then," said Celso. "*Adiós, mañeca.*" His *adiós* was a good-bye this time, and it sounded large. "And don't be afraid," he said. He said it softly, at Cuca. But he meant it for Rosa as well.

"Afraid of what?" asked Rosa. It was not a pointed question. It simply startled her.

"No, nothing, it's just that I have been wanting to come for a long time now, but she didn't want me to."

Rosa gave him a little bit of a smile, and he left.

Afterward Rosa said to Cuca, "All right, it's done. Let's see what your father says. And I think—well, the words are right. Don't be afraid. We should not be afraid in this house."

JOSÉ CAME home exactly at six, and Rosa told him.

"Who do you say came?" began José, his voice rising. "Well, I don't want him around here, this whatever he is, and if he comes I'm going to do it, run him off!"

"No," said Rosa. "You're not going to do that." She said this quietly, which is always very loud.

"Well. Then I'm not going to be here. At eight, you say? Well, I'm just not going to be here," and he got up from where he was sitting and left the house.

CELSO CAME, also exactly, at eight.

Chairs were taken out onto the porch, and they all sat and waited, talking a little, the younger sisters playing a game in the yard. Rosa fanned herself, and Cuca kept her head down.

Nine o'clock passed, and José did not return, and before ten, Cuca and her younger sisters could hardly stay awake.

"Doña Rosa," said Celso, who was like that, using the familiar rather than the formal, "Doña Rosa, go ahead and go to bed. All of you. I know it's late for everyone."

"But it's possible," said Rosa, "that he won't come back until morning."

"The hour doesn't matter," said Celso. "I will wait for him here. You take everyone to sleep. You can close the door if you like, but I'm going to wait."

"No, it's all right, of course. I'll leave the door open." But with that she did gather everyone, including Cuca, and took them inside to bed.

Of course, no one could sleep, and there was a great deal of whispering and shushing. José did not come and he did not come, until after eleven or twelve, sometime beyond counting, when he finally came to the porch and headed toward the door.

"Sir, I would like to speak with you."

José had not seen him or had not wanted to see him. His mouth fared no better than his eyes, and all José could muster was, "In a minute, in a minute, excuse me."

Nobody knew what to think. Rosa had lain down with the two younger girls, and Cuca and Amparo were simply quiet. It looked like the jungle in the house, so many open eyes in the night.

José came in, crossed the room almost running, and went out the back door to the outhouse. It was in a far corner of the yard, and he entered, sat, and closed the door.

A great deal of time passed, time that did not want to be counted. Rosa finally got up and said to no one in particular— which meant to everyone, as they were all awake—"What's wrong with this man, not coming out from the toilet? This ridiculousness, whatever he is doing, I don't understand."

They could hear Celso still outside moving around in his chair. Rosa went outside and said to Celso, "José will be out in a minute, I'm sure." And then she went back into the house and followed José's tracks to the outside.

"José! José!" Rosa stood outside the outhouse door.

"What, what's wrong?" said José from somewhere inside.

"Come out, come on, this boy is waiting for you still."

José simply cleared his throat, and she did not want to create a fuss out there by the toilet. She went back into the house but was embarrassed to go out and tell Celso what was happening, so she waited inside. Waiting seemed to be the thing.

But finally she could not wait anymore. She slipped back to the outhouse a second time. "José, come out of there, come on! Look, or I'm going to tell this boy to come out here to you. If you don't come out, that's what I'm going to tell him."

José opened the door, pretending to fix his pants. He did not say anything. Everyone in the house was looking out the back window. He walked through the house, and came to the front door, and opened it.

Celso didn't wait.

"Don José, I come to speak to you, to say I have honorable intentions toward your daughter. Where is Doña Rosa? I would like to speak with her as well."

It was hard at that moment not to include her, as she was right behind José, keeping him from coming back in. *"Vieja,"* said José, *"vieja,* come out here."

Rosa came out and stood next to him. "What do you want?" said Rosa to José, but it was just something to say.

Celso answered instead. "I would like to speak to the both of you. I know that you've been told things about me, and they are true. But I come so that you can meet me for yourselves. So that you can see what I was, and who I am now, and what I am going to be. I want you to know me all the way. I have honorable intentions toward the *mañeca,* and I want to marry her.

"I know you've probably heard that I have been a ladies' man, that I've had many girlfriends, and that I've never married any of them. It's true. But I want to marry now, and quickly. She is the one for me."

Cuca waited for her father to throw Celso out of the yard, perhaps over the fence.

Instead José said, "I'm prepared. You will be a good son-in-law, and I am ready to act accordingly. Come over anytime you want; you will be welcome."

Rosa and Celso looked hard at José, and the girls tried to get a good look through the window. One did not see this sort of miracle every day.

"Anytime," said José.

NO ONE COULD explain it, and no one wanted to ask. José just sometimes would make up his mind that way about things, no matter what had come before. Who knew what had happened in the outhouse.

Celso came around the next afternoon and took Cuca and Amparo out to the movies, joining up with Rafael, who, after being told what had happened and with what success, decided that this night would be his turn.

Celso tried to tease him into going over to the house right away instead of going to the movies, but Rafael thought the better of it. After the movies, later. That's when.

"I don't know," said Celso. "I think it will have been a mistake not to go while it's still early in the day. This family, they make you wait a lot!"

What Rafael didn't know was that Amparo had already spoken to her parents about him, and José had thrown up his arms but hadn't argued.

"Two in a row," he said, "just like that. Are we running a sale here, Rosa?"

But Amparo was different, after all. She was older and had already been married. It was a courtesy from the centuries, and she wanted to ask the blessing of her parents this time, to see if things might work better in this manner. She had run away once, but now she wanted to stay. She wanted for herself and Rafael, for the both of them, to be able to stay.

Rafael was all big talk throughout the evening, very brave, and it made Amparo laugh to know what she already knew.

Amparo suggested that they plan to leave the movies early, if he wanted, so that they could arrive at her house before her parents went to sleep. The family had had enough late evenings all wrapped up into the night before.

The four of them got back to the house about half-past eight that evening, and Celso said to Rafael, "Well, I beat you, ha. But now it's your turn."

They could see José through the window, drinking a weak coffee. The four of them went right through the gate, up the walk, and into the house. Just like that.

Amparo said, "*Mamá,* I've brought a boy here who wants to see you." She was talking to Rosa and José both. It was just easier to say only *Mamá.* Who can explain about these things.

"Yes," said Rafael. "What I'd like is to visit, in the manner of my friend here." He nodded at Celso. There was a great deal in that nod.

"It's rude, I think, the four of us," said Celso to everyone, "that we stand around the street corner out there instead of coming into the yard. We have no wish to be rude, certainly, do you think, Doña Rosa?"

José did not say much, but he didn't have to this time. He simply nodded his head in a yes, more or less.

Rosa said for the both of them, in words, "Yes, it's all right. That makes sense."

So it was agreed, everyone could visit everyone. Just like that. The matter was a small one and did not take much time.

CELSO AND Cuca planned their wedding, and it was a regular story.

Amparo was ready to marry Rafael as well, and they had informed everyone and done all the necessary visiting of relatives.

The four of them began the ritual of Saturday nights and Sunday afternoons together, and for the next months it was good.

Things went so well, in fact, and with his mother, Doña Manuela, liking Amparo very much, Rafael and Amparo decided to have their wedding even before Cuca and Celso.

"What a surprise party that was," Amparo would say over and again, talking about the party at which they had first met. "What a surprise."

It was only one surprise among many, however.

Rafael had a girlfriend before Amparo, whom he had been seeing for a while and with whom he had spent some time on the ranch before coming into town for the surprise party. They had not lived together nor made promises, but she nonetheless followed Rafael around, and in fact he had not expected her at all on the ranch.

She learned about Amparo, and she began to follow the two of them on their evenings and afternoons. Amparo was so much in love, she could only see Rafael.

On a Sunday afternoon Amparo, Rafael, Cuca, and Celso had gone to the *cortina* of trees to witness the passing of another fine weekend, to breathe in something from the great gardens, when suddenly a small taxi pulled up along the street in front of them.

From its window this same woman began to shout, "Rafael!"

They all looked at her.

"Rafael, aha! This is just the way I wanted to catch you. You tell her right now," this woman said, pointing at Amparo, "that I'm the one you love and that we have stayed together—she will know how. . . . "

"Rafael," said Amparo, "someone is speaking to you." Amparo got up from the bench to leave, and Cuca got up because what else could she do? Celso placed himself between the two women, gathered their arms in his, and began to walk them along the trees.

"That Lamberto Díaz," he said, "these gardens. Everything so green. Have I ever told you about Lázaro Luna and his part in these gardens? He was a friend of your father's."

It was Celso's way of being quiet, of being silent for them all, by talking.

Rafael stayed seated on the bench, dispirited, with his head down and without breath. The woman did not come out of the taxi but continued to shout at him from the doorway of the car.

"You've got to come home now, we've got things to take care of, I've missed you, Rafael. . . . "

Rafael could move only along the line of her voice, as if it lifted him onto it and carried him to the door of the taxi. He could not lift his head, and something in his legs gave way, or he had no legs, so that he half fell into the taxi before he knew it, before any of them knew it, and the taxi drove off.

AMPARO TURNED to look at Rafael, but he had gone.

There was a circus in town, in a manner of speaking. The circus when it came through town now and then had some attractions that were so popular, some small amazements, that finally the town made a permanent place for these parts of the circus and did not let them go. It became a section of town unto itself, in between the regular part of Cajeme and the Plano Oriente, and accessible only by following the *cortina* of trees through the great garden, which they did.

Celso wanted to keep their minds off what had happened, as no one knew yet exactly what in fact had happened, and he steered Cuca and Amparo in the direction of the circus amusements, toward some of the games or for some pig cookies perhaps. Anything.

Amparo blurted out, "He must be married! That must be his wife who had come to find him—"

"But how could he be married, Ampi?" said Celso, referring to her as if he were her own sister. "How could he be, with Doña Manuela liking you so much? She would have said something. We all would have known."

"Who knows the secret life of a man?" said Amparo.

"No, he's not married. He's in love with you, and you will be married."

The tag of words went back and forth between them, and all Cuca could do was feel sorry.

"Come here, come on, sister-in-law," said Celso, "we'll go to the games here. You'll feel better." And they all tried to feel better.

But in the air the circus played its music, and popular in those days was the old song "Amor Perdido," lost love. It would not stop. *Amor perdidooo,* went the music, and Celso mimicked it, *"Ay, amor perdiiidooo,"* and he tried to make her laugh, but she could not.

"Oh, he'll come back. Of course he will."

Amparo would never forget the song, and she would live this moment many times for the rest of her life. *"Amor perdido,"* she would say in a whisper, like Cuca saying the Act of Contrition, "it's like that, that's what it does to you." For Amparo the song would be better than onions for bringing water to her face.

DOÑA MANUELA told Amparo the next day, "Yes. Well, Rafael has been seeing this woman for eight years. But she's from, well," and she nodded in the direction of the Plano Oriente part of town. "I'm sure," she said, "that when you marry him . . ."

"No," said Amparo, "I don't think it will happen."

And for a while, no one saw Rafael.

Amparo wrote a letter to her aunt Carmelita, whom she had not seen for years, and said that she wanted to come to Nogales to stay for a while.

Amparo wasn't sure why she did it, just that Nogales—and everything it was for her—seemed part of another lifetime, and Carmelita would not therefore be able to remind her of Rafael. Carmelita was as far from Rafael as was humanly possible in this world, and it was where she wanted to be.

"Come," said Carmelita in her letter that sounded like a voice and came right back, oh yes, "please come. We have so much to talk about. I have missed you, and I have work for you, so you must come right away. I know where there is good work." Amparo's world was spinning, and Carmelita's purring voice made the whole matter feel like a hypnotist's wheel, a calm voice telling her what to do, how to get out of this mess.

As much as it was confusion, this decision was also an act of spite on Amparo's part, saying, "I don't want to see him anymore; how could he do this to me?" She was capable of these kinds of big decisions. It ran in her family.

Amparo accepted Carmelita's invitation because it was the last thing on earth she ever thought she would do and the last thing anyone could believe. That made it right. That was the measure of what she felt. The whole thing, her whole life, was clear: she resided in the impossible. So why not?

That was what she said. But Amparo felt sure Rafael would come back and that he would look for her. As angry and as sad as she was, she at least felt sure of that. No matter what she said.

Rafael did come back. And he did look for her, and he wrote many letters, pleading with her for any answer at all. And he went to Nogales to find her. "Amparo, please," his letters would all begin.

"BUT DOÑA Carmelita," Rafael said, "I have heard she came here."

"No, you are mistaken. I'm sorry."

"But the letters I wrote, did they find her?"

"All the letters arrived," she said.

And that was that.

When Amparo had said on the first day of her arrival that if Rafael were to call not to say she was here, Carmelita took her at her word. How could she not? she would later say. It was the only moral thing to do.

And so as not to bother Amparo, neither did Carmelita mention—as they would surely have upset Amparo, and who would want that?—any of the letters, even as they continued to arrive after years, or the encounter with Rafael when he had come looking for her.

After a week or so, in Cajeme, Rosa told Rafael where Amparo had gone. Though Amparo had told Rosa not to give Rafael the address, Rosa knew something about these things. And she knew her daughter.

But so did Carmelita.

AMPARO WAITED to come back to Cajeme and never unpacked everything. During this time Cuca and Celso married, and Amparo was her bridesmaid. Amparo said nothing to them about Rafael. He had come by later to congratulate Celso and Cuca and to say that he had written many letters, and that he had gone to Nogales to look for Amparo and had gone to where she worked but could not find her.

Cuca thought that Amparo must not want to see him any longer, and so she did not say anything. She did not want to be rude. She wanted to be Amparo's friend, and so she was quiet.

Carmelita wrote regularly now and said that Amparo, of course, was happy with her in Nogales, and popular, and that she was starting to see a boy, and that all was well. And more about the boy, and regular things.

And Amparo had in fact found a boy, a thin one, Pedro. And after a while, finally she married him. But it was too much, living alone together in Nogales—which is how they felt, that they were living alone, Carmelita not counting for as much as she once did. That is what they thought.

So they moved without her to Guaymas, where Pedro's family was, having come there from years on the sea.

MANY YEARS later, Pedro's sister lived in Cajeme, and he and Amparo would make the visit to see everyone.

To herself Amparo thought, how much, one of these times, she would have liked to see Rafael once more. It didn't matter that she was married to Pedro. She could not help thinking such a thing. It would not go away.

And one day she found him at the everything store, El Todo, buying seeds.

"Ampi, it's you."

Amparo had pretended through the years that she had not, but every time she was in the town she had asked about him. She could have come on the bus to see Pedro's sister, she could say. She thought of a great many other reasons. If just one day she could see him. Amparo painted him still as she had known him, young, hers from the first moment at the surprise party.

She was in the store asking for a demonstration of an appliance when she saw two men lifting down some heavy bags of seed. He was in the penumbra shadows of the small store, in a corner and without much light from the window or the small bulb.

He turned when he heard her voice.

"Ampi, it's you," he said, and he came to her and he hugged her. And they hugged each other again, with arms and with a laughter.

He told her he had married and that he had grown sons, both at the universities, of Arizona and Sonora. "Who would have thought, so smart. And they have been good boys to me."

"I am married too," she said, and a few other things.

"Will you come out to eat with me, some lunch?"

"I'm sorry, no. There are people waiting for me. You know." It was too much all at once.

"These sons," he said, "they would have been yours if you had answered the letters."

"The letters?"

"The ones I sent you, and I went to look for you as well. Where did you hide, Ampi?" He shrugged his shoulders to ask the question. "Why did you do it? I wanted to explain." His voice was a low sound.

Amparo thought, So this is how much a trip to the store that has everything costs.

"Some lives," she said, "they're like this."